Potomac Review

Potomac Review is a journal of fiction, poetry, and nonfiction
published by the Paul Peck Humanities Institute at
Montgomery College, Rockville
51 Mannakee Street, Rockville, MD 20850

Potomac Review has been made possible through
the generosity of Montgomery College.

A special thanks to Dean Rodney Redmond.

For submission guidelines and more information:
www.potomacreview.org

Potomac Review, Inc. is a not-for-profit 501 c(3) corp.
Member, Council of Literary Magazines & Presses
Indexed by the American Humanities Index
ISBN: 978-0-9990403-4-8
ISSN: 1073-1989

SUBSCRIBE TO POTOMAC REVIEW
One year at $24 (2 issues)
Two years at $36 (4 issues)
Sample copy order, $12 (single issue)

TABLE OF CONTENTS

FICTION

POETRY

NONFICTION

"I'm gonna be here from now on," she said,
tightening her ponytail.

ANOTHER STRANGE LAND

Sour yeast, the cloy of it, still hung in the air after mass that morning. Bailey's eyes and nose ran from the fire of Pine-Sol, his skin crawling in a relentless web since the cusp of sunrise, when he and Nan discovered sourdough starter bubbling down the cabinets and onto their linoleum. Nan had sent a swearword in Bailey's direction, hobbling past the mess in kitten heels and a jean dress patched sickly with their own floral drapes. Mass took precedent.

For a long while after church, after cleaning gluten sludge and crust with sore and skinny arms, Bailey stood in the doorway of the country farmhouse. His nails peeled at the chipped doorframe—painted over so many times with shades of *eggshell* it felt thick and gummy—and he once again wondered what color he'd find if he drew a knife right through its middle and peered inside. Like it had an abdomen. But he was no surgeon.

He liked the place all right. It was a relic of former beauty, the left side of its structure leaning, panels dirty white, all but one of its windows smeared in fog. He'd thought of leaving before, of running the length of their broken driveway and disappearing into the narrow rivers of Hinton.

Nan beckoned him from her armchair. "Toss me some pork rinds and I'll give you a nickel."

Their pantry stood two strides away from Nan, but she was already sitting. Bailey lodged his arm elbow-deep in the bin and handed her the foul snack, his face turning. She ripped it open like a confetti popper, laughing loud as she hunkered over to pick up the nearly weightless puffs scattered across their tartan carpet.

1

She stepped on several in the process, ate some straight from the floor, and sank back into the dregs of her chair. She hacked and flipped on the radio. Bluegrass jumped and crackled.

It wasn't just Nan's slovenly love for baking, or the way she took her car rides, smoking Americans with the windows sealed shut (she'd always *just* had her hair set), or the way she never stopped chattering until the question of Mom came up, whom she'd seen the very worst of, the very end of, and she'd still not entertain a moment of reminiscing. It was everything she did and didn't do that left Bailey peeling at door frames. He often found himself bent over a syrupy stain or following sharp crumbs from the kitchen counter to the innards of Nan's recliner. He'd fish for chewed-over peanut shells in the depths of its pleather seat, coming eye-level with the chair's curling arm, the whole thing pocked with cigar burns.

"You wouldn't know a good Cuban if it burnt ya," Nan would say, taking a fat mouthful of smoke and spouting it toward the ceiling light. With her knobby index finger, she'd trace the tobacco scabs on the leather.

She'd never had a real Cuban cigar. Just the ones Jim Trace sold her when he was likely loose on cash. He'd even put them in shoe boxes of coffee beans, rolled them in soft linen—fresh from the Black Market. He really put on a show for Nan. Bailey was always sent to collect the fine new products from Jim. Jim would leer at him, hand over the box. Jim was shaggy, his face set and savage. Termites had likely had a go at him once or twice—he always smelled like a pine box.

The fence dividing the properties of Jim Trace and Nan marked Bailey's refuge, just a short stretch of grass where the two acreages touched, a few hundred feet lined with enormous poplar trees and berry bushes. It was far from the farmhouse, poised at the top of a steep slope that made Bailey's calves burn and weep. When standing there, he could see. The hills that rose and dipped and lilted, treetops like shag carpet, the gray curve of

Hinton's only road. Smoke pluming from a coal train far away. The vantage point was untouchable, a window. Things were in order. But he liked it most because of Mia.

Fresh folks were rare in Hinton. At best, the place had a few hundred residents that would've been a lot less bitter had the coal stuck around. But when someone new came along, Bailey always found out. He listened shamelessly in the aisles of Leroy's Market, gossip drifting over shelves of canned soup and vegetables. He listened at the middle school, the soda shop, at the edges of the deserted mine — a crater where kids smoked and drank and dropped rocks miles down into darkness. He'd even follow them to the quarry, on occasion, where five had died just that year. But no word of newcomers, not for a long time, and when he happened across Mia while picking blackberries, his fingers stained bright violet, he froze. She had a short torso and Rockette legs, fingernails covered in Band-Aids and a curve to her posture that made one shoulder just a little lower than the next.

He asked who are you and what are you doing out here, not caring much to hide his callous tone. She stood at the edge of the fence studying him like a fish in a glass bowl. Her eyes were too big for her face.

"I'm Jim Trace's nephew — Mia," she said, leaning against the wooden stakes and sticking her hand out.

Bailey looked at the blue and green Band-Aids, and then to her chest. "You're a girl."

She let her hand drop. "Yeah."

"So you're no nephew."

Mia rolled her eyes hard. "You're rude," she said. And she smiled. "You mind?" She gestured toward Bailey's side of the fence.

Bailey shifted, unable to take his eyes off her hands, the Band-Aids and her odd body. He said all right, setting down his

3

bucket, and Mia grinned as she shifted one of the loose stakes and shimmied through.

For a while they sat across from one another eating blackberries, Mia making crude jokes while Bailey braided tall strands of grass between his fingers. She told him she'd come to Hinton for the summer because her mom was getting married to a man Mia said was like meat with eyeballs. She had a quick and wild way of speaking that ached the space behind Bailey's eyes.

"His favorite food is green beans from the can," Mia said. She peeled a Band-Aid off her pinky and resealed it tighter. "He does those stupid math games in the newspaper and his wallet is made of Duct Tape."

"Is he mean to you or something?" Bailey asked.

"No, he's nice enough."

"So why do you care?"

She gave Bailey another big-eyed onceover. "He's boring. That's worse."

Bailey watched her rifle through the bucket, probably grasping for more of the plumpest berries, before he looked back out at the valley.

"So what're the people like here?" Mia asked. Purple teeth.

Bailey snorted. Most of the kids in town were either halfway illiterate or rich, and the rest were just Amish. He knew for one thing that he wasn't dumb or rich, and he wasn't about to be whittling benches, so he'd been content to keep to himself in Hinton. He helped Nan around the farm and worked through his encyclopedias. He'd never had someone to share a bucket of berries with, and it wasn't so bad, really, but he wasn't sure he'd be any good for it.

"Nothing to write home about," he said. "So, how'd you end up so far up Jim's property?" He ran his fingers up the rope of grass he'd fixed and grinned at the texture.

Mia's shoulders teetered and she pointed her blue thumb towards the oak on the other side of the fence. It was both full and budding, breaching above the weaker trees around it. "Jim went hunting and I thought I'd finally check out that old thing he never shuts up about at Thanksgiving."

"A tree?"

"Half my family line's buried right here," she said.

Bailey stared at the base of its trunk and watched the grass shudder and settle. "Why are all their graves unmarked?" he asked.

Mia threw a blackberry in her mouth and smiled big, a weird purply crime scene. "Doesn't really matter much," she said. "Not like they're here to see it."

In the distance, Bailey could hear his grandmother ringing the dinner bell and hooves shuddering the earth. "Supper," he said, standing up and scanning his jeans for dirt.

Mia stood too, scooping out one last handful of blackberries from the bucket. He felt her watching him as she swallowed too many berries at once. "Same time tomorrow?"

He stared at her.

She gave another glance at his jeans, her mouth scrunching slightly. "I'm gonna be here from now on," she said, tightening her ponytail.

"What's that got to do with me?" It was half-hearted.

Mia's mouth tightened. "I've never had many friends, and I'd be willing to bet you haven't, either."

Bailey's ears went hot and tingling, so he looked back down the hill.

She paused for a moment, wrinkling her nose like she might sneeze, her thin lips twisting to the side. She slipped back through the fence.

Every night that summer Bailey hiked up to where the two properties met so he could see the girl with the Band-Aid hands. She was constantly disheveled, dirty even, seeming to notice how much it irritated him, her bandages often flapping off to show raw fingertips. Sometimes she'd tell him outlandish stories of world travel that he suspected were lies, but he found himself unbothered. She was full-of-it, but she wasn't boring.

Most days, after meeting at the fence, Mia took off across Bailey's property as if it were her own—a place she'd grown up and knew backwards and forwards, like the sun burned into her eyelids. She led Bailey in elaborate circles until he had fat blisters on his toes, markers of more time spent roaming his home than he ever had—or wanted to.

"Hang on," he said one afternoon, leaning against a boulder and pulling off his left boot. They'd been walking for hours, Mia always six steps ahead and pointing her Swiss Army knife at unsuspecting trees.

When they stopped, Mia slouched, her lips pursing, though she seemed to hold back—her gaze on Bailey's swollen foot. She reached into her pocket and withdrew a handful of colorful Band-Aids. He took two.

Mia waved him off, leaning against the boulder and crossing her arms. "You've lived on this big farm your whole life and never explored it."

Bailey concentrated on wrapping the Band-Aids tightly around his toes.

"I grew up in a huge city," said Mia, shaking her head. "If I had all this, I'd probably be a lot tamer." She swatted a fly. "You know, get all my energy out. If I got to grow up here like you—"

"I didn't really grow up here."

She looked at him. "Oh, I just figured. It seems like most of the people around here have been in for the long haul."

"Most of them have." Bailey slid his boot back on and checked his pants and shirt for bramble.

"Why'd you come here then?" she asked.

"To live with my grandma," Bailey said. "Let's go." Mia watched him for a moment before setting off again. He followed, a slight limp to put up with, and pointlessly hoped she would slow down.

She didn't. After traversing two brooks and his late grandpa's slaughtering barn, Bailey rounded the side of the hill to find Mia standing at the cusp of the pond, her hands pressed against the backs of her hips, her shoulder blades rolling close. Bailey followed her gaze to the milky water at her boots. A bull moaned from across the way, swinging his rope of a tail.

"Let's get in," Mia said.

"You're joking."

"I'm not."

"It's full of cow shit."

Mia pressed her lips. "My Aunt Tracy says it's good for your skin."

"Shit?"

"Are you coming or not?" she asked.

For a moment, he entertained it. Sweat pooled in every crevice of his body. He imagined the coolness of the water. A splash, a cleanse, but then—hairs caked in mud, crust under his nails, bacteria wandering. He moved away, and Mia's eyes followed.

"I'll just be a minute," Mia said, stepping out of her oversized boots and pressing them into his hands. She unbuttoned her shorts just above the bellybutton and slid them off. Bailey's face lit and he looked away. She tossed them at his head and laughed. "Quit bugging."

He burned hotter, turning back just as she sprang into the water. Drooping, oblong shadows of yellow and amethyst marked her ribs and lower back. Bailey's eyes locked on those shadows, if only for the time she was propelled in the air. Old bruises, weeks old, healing. It was shocking, brutal. It made him sweat an entirely different kind of sweat. He didn't want to know who had given them to her. Bailey nudged around the mud with the toe of his sneaker until it made the shape of a llama.

Mia surfaced, scrubbing the dirt from above her eyebrows, chin, and ears, her blonde hair soaked against her head.

"You just want to cool down?" Bailey asked.

Mia flicked water at his feet. "I needed a bath. Haven't had one in a while." She laughed and began floating on her back, the tips of her toes and belly breaching the surface.

"What, Jim doesn't own a tub?" It was facetious, but Bailey thought, actually, it wouldn't be so out of character.

"Why would I do it inside when I could do it out here?"

He watched her emerge from the water and waited a moment before handing over her boots. She wasn't close to dry, but still they headed onward, Bailey side-stepping the wayward droplets that flew from Mia's ponytail. Just when they reached the southern edge of his property, Mia snorting from laughter over some sort of *you had to be there* memory, Bailey spotted a familiar figure limping up the road.

Jim Trace wasn't the friendliest man in Hinton, but he was an honest farmer and a decent shot during deer season. He wasn't such an honest Black Market salesman, but to Bailey, the whole thing only made Jim more clever. His lurching, unsteady gait, said to be from a gunshot to the hip, made him a spectacle around town, but his home doubled as a fresh produce stand in winter and he offered fair prices for unusual stuff. Bailey figured Nan took a liking to Jim long before Bailey was in the picture.

"Wonder where he's coming from," Bailey said.

Mia's laughter clipped off. "Not sure, but it's getting kinda late," she said, looking over her shoulder at the top of the hill. "I should probably get back."

Bailey watched her, waiting a moment before replying.

"You don't want to go talk to Jim?"

"No, I should head back." She turned quick and walked toward the fence, Bailey struggling to match her pace.

"Something wrong?" he asked, reaching out to touch her shoulder.

She halted and threw off his hand. "Buzz off." She turned red and looked at her shoes. "Don't do that."

Bailey didn't move, and after a moment, Mia seemed to soften, her eyes flicking back to the road. She apologized under her breath and tucked her damp hair behind her ears. "It's nothing. Jim just likes me back by dinner. I should go."

Bailey nodded as she departed, watching her ascend the slope until she was doll-sized.

Bailey loved the way his encyclopedias smelled. They were old, peeling. They reeked of sap and ash. Each volume was unique, a rip shaped like lightning in L, grass and dirt from a pressed clover in B, Mom's inky annotations in R.

After a long day reading P—notable words: palaeobotany, pariah, and Pityriasis Versicolor—he heard a guttural sound from downstairs. He ran down to find Nan yelling out the window at a too-tall girl who sat smiling on the gasoline tank, arms draping over the edge of the fence, a big mare nibbling at her palm.

"The hell you doing on my tank?" Nan said, tossing a rancid dishrag into the sink. Bailey watched as damp flecks of bread flung onto the counter. She'd wrenched the window open to its hilt.

"I'm just sitting," said Mia.

"Well get out," Nan said. "You ain't gonna find pot out here, so get off my tank. Go on."

"She's not looking for pot," said Bailey, tossing a filthy paper towel into the garbage. "That's Jim Trace's niece."

Nan looked back and forth between them. "Jim Trace ain't got no family."

Mia waved her bandaged fingers. "He's my uncle."

Bailey shook his head. "It's fine, go back into the living room, she's just here to see me."

Nan stared at him, studied him up and over like it was some sort of trick before she gave a *to-hell-with-it* sigh and walked back to her armchair.

"You got condoms?" she called gruffly.

Bailey slammed a cabinet. "Thought you were a Catholic," he

quipped back. He looked out the window and apologized to Mia.

"Guess Jim doesn't mention me much," said Mia with a half-smile, scratching at her neck.

"What are you doing here?" Bailey asked.

"Wanted to hangout. Wanted to see where you live."

Bailey considered this. "I can't right now," he said.

Mia slid off the tank and stepped toward the window. "Why's that?"

He looked at her, his fingernails digging into the sides of his jeans.

"So you don't have visitors often," said Mia, leaning against the sill. "Give me a shot, will you? I'm not gonna rearrange your knickknacks or hide your underwear."

Bailey stood still for a moment before unlocking the back door. He didn't breathe as Mia stepped inside. He watched as her eyes scanning the cramped space. She took another step before stopping cold, glancing his way. She slid off her boots and set them outside. "Sorry," she said.

With only two small bedrooms and a study it took no time for Bailey to walk her through the house, moving quickly past Nan, who was already snoring.

"She should probably get her throat checked," Mia said as they walked upstairs. She actually seemed worried. "She sounds like a beat engine."

"She's a pack a day," Bailey said. He slept with bright orange earplugs every night. "Here's Nan's place." He pushed open the door at the end of the hallway. It gave way to a room with heavy floral drapes and a matching bedspread. It reeked of potpourri and menthol cigarettes, and, on that particular day, some kind of cured meat.

"Well, she seems to keep it in order," Mia said, running her hand over Nan's armoire. When she reached the end of the cabinet, she gasped at the black dust that coated her palm.

Bailey shook his head. "It's disgusting."

Mia nodded, her mouth twisting into a smile. She swiped her hand over Nan's bedspread. "By your standards or mine?"

Bailey chewed the inside of his cheek and gestured Mia back into the hall. He swung the door shut.

"So, do I get to see your corner of this place?" Mia asked.

Bailey rubbed the back of his neck until it burned. He was blistering inside. "I mean, it's just a bedroom. Nothing to see."

Mia watched him for moment, her smile fading. She asked what was wrong, crossing her arms, defensive. The sight almost made Bailey laugh, but unease rose over him again.

"My mom spent a lot of time in there. It was our room." He dug his fingernails into the heels of his hands, thinking. "And then it was her sickroom. Now it's just mine."

Mia stepped in front of him, her fingers twirling together as if she wanted to touch him. She reached into her pocket and withdrew a braided chain of grass. She held it up and it flopped sadly over her knuckles like the neck of a dead goose. "Here," she said, putting it in his hand. "It calms you down, right?"

He took the rope of grass and looked at her, running his palm along the textured cable.

"You always do that when you're bugging out," she said. "I started carrying it around for when I get a little worked up, too." She reached out her hand and ran a finger over the braid. "It's not really the same because of all these." She wiggled her colorful fingers.

"Come on," Bailey said, pocketing the braid.

When he opened his bedroom door, he looked mostly at Mia. She would see the three windows streaked with cleaner. His twin bed, made neat by a sterile white sheet. The desk that doubled as a shelf for hundreds of books placed in size and color order. The basket of dust cloths and baking soda and vinegar and a shelf of his mother's things. Little porcelain horses, her wedding band, a book about sailing. The room smelled of nothing, but that was sort of something.

11

Mia walked right to his bedside table where a record player sat proud. "This is really cool," she said, running her hands over the ribbed plate.

"You don't already have one?" asked Bailey.

Mia pulled her hand away. "Yeah, well, we always used my dad's but he took it when he left." She picked at a Band-Aid. "Mom doesn't like me listening to music. She's a drag, you know. I've always wanted one."

Bailey watched her scratch repeatedly at the tip of her pointer finger. "I've only got The Beatles on vinyl," he said. "You want to listen?"

Her mouth dropped open. "Only The Beatles?" She laughed. "Are you bugging again? Of course."

He let the needle down to meet its rotating mate. His speakers crackled, tinny.

"I'm gonna marry John Lennon," Mia said, tracing her fingers around the outside edges of *Sgt. Pepper's Lonely Hearts Club Band*. Her eyes devoured its colorful chaos.

"I think Yoko would put up a fair fight," said Bailey.

Mia ignored him, her blue forefinger now landing on a darker, laughing face among the masses. "Fred Astaire," she said, jabbing her finger. "And that's Einstein and Miss Marilyn Monroe . . . and there—" She halted, her finger just beneath the chin of a serious, rounded face. "That's him. That's my dad's favorite poet. Dylan Thomas." The corners of her eyes crinkled as she held up the cover to catch the clean, white sunshine pouring into Bailey's room.

"Do not go gentle into that good night," Bailey offered.

Mia's eyes darted to him, shining, but Bailey shrugged, taking the cover and sliding the vinyl back inside.

On the way out, they paused in the study so Mia could take in the mass of encyclopedias lining the room. She gazed over the gilded letters before withdrawing a volume and slouching into the green armchair. She opened the book and let the pages pour down, her eyes scanning the bolded words.

Bailey stuck his finger between two pages to stop the flow, pointing to the middle. "Paros," he said, glancing over the description he'd recently read. "It's an island in Greece. I'd like to go someday."

Mia looked up at him. "I've been," she said.

"You have?"

She nodded. "You'd like it. It's clean."

Later that evening, they walked to the underbelly of the hill and sat still, Mia's legs crossed like origami and sweat rolling down the craters of her collarbones. The air was thick and sultry, cradling the trill of locusts as Bailey watched her crush a mosquito on her thigh and wipe her hand on the grass. She let her head hang back, the sky lighting a garish pink before it flashed back to night again and again.

Bailey shifted, leaning against the incline of the hill as Mia peeled the tin top off a can of peanuts. It was silent for a while as they sat there, but Mia didn't let it go on for long. She whipped around, a peanut flying from her hand.

"Can we play a game?" she asked.

"Like Tag?"

"No, not like that—not a game, game," she said.

"Well, what is it?"

"It's like a free pass," Mia said, kicking out and crossing her ankles, "so long as we both agree on it."

"OK."

"Good."

Bailey stared at her. "What's this all about?"

"The idea is we both get to ask one question, just one, and the person's gotta answer honestly."

"Why?"

Her face tightened. "Because what's the point if you're just gonna lie?" she said.

Bailey pinched the bridge of his nose. "No, I mean, why play?"

13

"I just want to understand you better," she said, crunching a nut with her canine tooth.

Bailey doubted her words but chose not to care. "One free pass?"

"You got it."

Bailey pulled at a thread on his sleeve. "All right," he said, sitting up straighter. "What's with the Band-Aids?"

Her eyes perked in disbelief. "Seriously?"

"What?"

She laughed, leaning back on her elbows again, but it wasn't a warm laugh, or even a real one. "You get one free pass and you wanna know about my stupid fingers," she said, rubbing her eyes. They were red from hay fever. "All right, I'll tell you." She peeled off a Band-Aid and stuck it to her knee, jabbing out her pointer finger for Bailey to see the raw, stubby nail. "I've been biting them for ages," she said, observing it herself. "Mom says it's ugly like bad acne so I wear all these to keep them nice and pretty." She waggled her multicolored hands and gave a lifeless grin.

"And you can't stop?" he asked.

"Nope," she said, wrapping the blue bandage back around her finger. "Got me a ringworm once, if I'm being honest."

"I'm sorry."

She shrugged. "I had to take a pretty big pill."

Bailey looked at her. "I meant about your mom," he said. "I'm sorry she made you feel ugly."

Mia faltered, her shoulders slouching. She rubbed her eyes harder. "Thanks." She looked around, seemed to be thinking. "I don't care about pretty. I don't want pretty," she said, rubbing her side.

Bailey nodded, thought of the bruises under her ribs, and nodded on.

"So, it's my turn, then." She straightened up and drummed her fingers on her knobby red knee. "Since your mom's gone" — she gave a quick look in his direction — "I mean, what was she like?

You know, before."

Bailey ran his fingers through the grass. "Soft," he said. "She was soft."

"You mean, like, her hair?"

He frowned. "No, I mean—of course her hair was soft, and her skin and clothes and stuff," he said. "But she was quiet. Her voice used to make me think of cotton when I was little. Just soft."

Mia said nothing. She shredded a few blades of grass. "And your Nan—you like her all right?"

"She takes care of me," he said. "We're not close."

"She doesn't get your"—she paused—"you know, your situation, then?"

Bailey laughed. "She thinks I'm weird. And she definitely likes all the cleaning."

"Do you?" Mia asked.

Bailey looked down and picked at a hangnail. "I don't know that I hate it," he said. "But sometimes it's weird. Sometimes I don't have a choice. Like Nan will break a hip if I don't do something."

"Like what?" she asked.

Bailey ripped out the hangnail and watched his middle finger bloom red. "It's a lot of things. Like cracking my back a certain way, or washing things twice, or not letting my mind wander during prayer." He sat up straighter. "You know, like, I have to say the Apostle's Creed two times in my head if that happens, or I'll get sick." He considered how strange it all sounded out loud, like magic, but nothing fun. Just a string of rules he couldn't break. Was afraid to break. "Mom was the same," he added.

Mia said sorry, and she looked it.

"It's fine, I'm not sad about it anymore."

"What happened to her?"

"She got sick when I was a kid. She wouldn't go to the doctor."

"Why not?"

Bailey ripped out the grass he'd been stroking and tore the

blades into confetti. "She was too scared."

Mia nodded, her eyes drifting. Silence spread for a few moments before she looked up at him, her eyes perking. "But look," she said, "you've got quite a life story!" She smiled wide, showing her teeth even, like it was something she thought would make him beam, too.

But Bailey looked away, chewing at the inside of his cheek and wishing for a shower. "I'd take Mom over a story," he said.

She blushed. "Yeah," she said, biting at the edge of her thumb. "I really am sorry." Then, silently, she touched his knee, and they sat together for a while longer.

A few days later, Bailey watched out the kitchen window as unseasonably cold rain washed over the farm. He found himself thankful for the downpour, as such days kept Mia from making him explore, but today she hadn't shown up at all. Not on his gas tank or slipping in through the back door, shaking out her damp hair like a mutt back from mischief. It was quiet in the farmhouse, sourdough rising lazily under a cheesecloth, Nan's cuckoo clock ticking ever closer to the hour. It was the first day in two weeks without Mia, and Bailey felt itchy and alone in his head. He longed for her company, and for a moment he was afraid she was bored of him.

That night, Bailey listened to music while he tried to sleep, mindlessly watching the black vinyl spin and wobble on the damaged plate. When the record scratched to a stop, he did not lift the needle. He'd heard something outside. Another short rap on the window sent him jolting upright, and there she was, wet and shrunken in her own silhouette. She was perched on the roofing just outside his room, her fingers prying at the windowsill as she tried to push it open. Bailey crossed the space in three steps, unlocking the window and helping her through the frame. He handed her a towel from his closet.

"How'd you climb that?" he asked. He couldn't believe she'd

been able to make it up the slick piping.

She gave a small, wry smile as she wiped down her body, shivering hard enough to rattle. "I'm good at getting where I wanna be," she said.

Bailey stayed quiet before he found himself wondering just how long she'd really been on his roof. When he didn't respond, Mia flushed and tossed the damp towel in his lap. "Sorry to bug you so late," she said.

"Where were you?"

She shrugged, dragging the wicker desk chair across the room and plopping down. She straddled it, her elbow on its back. "I needed a bit of time to myself."

Bailey clenched his jaw and swiped the water droplets from his windowsill. "Well then why are you here?"

"I wanted to hang."

Bailey didn't respond, tugging a Hinton Blackberry Festival sweatshirt over his pajamas. "Hey, how about we make some pancakes or something?" Mia said, standing.

"It's eleven," Bailey said, turning to glare at her. It hit him then how gray she looked, how her cheeks sort of dented, how her eyes sagged with great purple hammocks. She wasn't really sitting so much as holding herself up. He wondered how much longer he could ignore it all. "Come on," he said, "I'll make us something."

Mia managed to eat eight syrup-drenched pancakes by the time Bailey had stacked three on his plate. She lounged on the kitchen counter with a sticky napkin crumpled in her hand, watching as Bailey carved off a bite with his fork.

"Are you still hungry?" he asked, meeting her gaze. "We've got some bacon in the fridge, probably."

She tossed her head, laughing. "I couldn't eat more if I tried," she said, but the words weren't full, and she chewed at her thumbnail, right through the blue Band-Aid.

"Bet Jim's not the best cook," he said.

"No," she replied. "Not really."

17

Bailey swirled the butter and syrup. He wondered, then, for the first time in real, solid thought, who she was.

The next day, Bailey met Mia at the bottom of the hill, his hands full with his grandpa's old camping gear.

"What's that for?" Mia asked, eyeing the nylon and spokes bundled in his arms. "Are you going somewhere?"

Bailey dropped the equipment in the space between them. "No," he said, "we're gonna camp."

She stared at him. "You want us to camp?" Bailey nodded, and Mia crossed her arms. "I don't think I can," she said. "I mean, your Nan would probably be upset."

"She doesn't need to know," he said. "And it's not like Jim would care, right?"

Mia paused, searching him. "Right," she replied. She knelt down and sifted through the materials. "Right," she repeated, this time with more energy. She beamed at him, her fingers stretching out the tent. "This is genius," she said, bouncing up.

Bailey returned her smile. "Knew you'd like it," he said.

"We'll make a bungalow — I've always wanted a bungalow." She paused, lifting the fabric so its fibers could catch sunshine. "No," she said, "it'll be a mansion." She ran around him, her eyes mapping the earth for the perfect spot. "We'll decorate it and all."

"It'll be our place," Bailey said.

"You can keep your books here."

"And your Band-Aids."

They watched each other for a moment. "Thanks," said Mia. Bailey smiled. "Let's get started, OK?"

That day they built it all up, stumbling over the spokes with skinny arms, mad with laughter, with thrill. Bailey stole magazines from Nan's bathroom and they cut out little pictures and words, taping phrases like *Mind the blackberries!* and *Danger!* across the inside walls. Bailey brought out *E*, *A*, and *Q* from his stash and they stacked the books with all the Band-Aid packages Mia had in her backpack. When they finished, they sat exhausted among the afghans from Bailey's living room, reading aloud excerpts from the *E* and laughing at the sillier words Mia had never heard of. She was trying to say *electroencephalograph* in one breath when the door to the tent zipped open.

"The hell is this?" said Nan. She was making a great effort to look down into the tent, her knees cracking as she bent over. "The hell you two in here for?"

"We were just hanging out," Bailey said.

"Look, we swear," said Mia, standing and taking the whole tent up a notch with her ponytail. She bent back down just as fast, glowing red.

"It's midnight," Nan said as she gestured them out. "You've got no reason to be in here this late unless you were planning to camp." She narrowed her eyes, lip quivering. "And you sure as hell didn't ask to do that." They looked at one another and stayed silent. Nan groaned, shaking her head. "All right, come inside. Now."

When they walked into the kitchen Nan sent Mia to Bailey's room and said not to come out until she came and got her. "You come out before then and I'll fry your ass in butter." Mia paled and darted off, Bailey's door shutting with a soft click moments later.

Bailey leaned against the kitchen counter, his hands squeezing at the plastic. "I'm sorry," he said, not looking at Nan. "I should've asked."

Nan pulled up a wooden chair from the table and sat down with a hefty creak. She looked him over, her small gray eyes digging into him as they so rarely did. Bailey fixed his gaze on his fingernails.

"You remind me of your mamma, acting like this." Bailey looked up as Nan shook her head and sawed a hand across her mouth. "I know that girl ain't staying with Jim Trace," she said. "Or, if she is, he ain't know it."

"I think she left home." Guilt seeped through him.

19

"A runaway," Nan said, shaking her head again. "Wonder where she's been staying."

They were silent for a while, Bailey listening to the cuckoo clock until he couldn't stand it. "I think she'll run away if I tell her I know," he said. "Please, if you don't say anything—"

Nan slammed her hand on the counter. "I'm not getting locked up for kidnapping some runner!"

Bailey leaned forward. "Nan, she's got shiners all over. Big ones around her back. Please."

Nan slid her fist from the counter, slouching back. "You like this girl?" she asked. Bailey nodded. Nan tugged at the neckline of her checkered shirt. She laughed to herself. "Well, you like having a friend, I guess. Most kids in this town ain't worth for shit," she said. "I won't say nothing."

Bailey nodded again, too nervous to speak.

"She seems to be doing fine for now, but I wanna make sure she's being fed decent," said Nan, standing up and sliding the chair under the table. She leaned against its back. "And she needs structure, so you bet your ass I'm putting you both to work."

"Of course." Bailey straightened. "We'll do whatever you want."

Nan waved a veiny hand in his direction. "I'm not your pimp, Bailey." She ripped open a bag of rinds. "First thing tomorrow you two are gonna paint the porch, got it?"

"First thing."

Nan bit down on a puff and studied him from across the counter. "All right, then," she said. She crunched another pork rind. "All right."

When Bailey entered his room a few minutes later, he found Mia sitting at the outermost edge of his bed, bouncing her leg so fast it was blurry. "So what's happening?" she asked, looking behind him. "What'd she say?"

Mia arrived bright and early the next morning, her hair tied back in a lopsided braid. They met in the kitchen where Nan handed off a pail of eggshell paint and two brushes, giving an unaffectionate grumble as she escorted them out to the wraparound porch, shutting the screen door. It didn't take long to get the hang of painting the wooden railings, but the sun was blazing with no respite of wind. After a while they rested beneath an arching poplar tree, taking big swigs from a gallon of water.

"Think she'd mind if we made a mark on this tree?" Mia asked, nudging Bailey's side.

Bailey snorted as he took a gulp, coughing as the water whipped down the wrong pipe. "Absolutely," he said. "What do you have in mind?"

Mia smiled and placed her palm gently on top of the open paint pail, lifting it to show a luminous white hand. She stood and observed the trunk for a moment before slapping it. She held her hand there, pressing hard and then releasing to reveal its signature. "You do it, too," she said.

Bailey was surprised at how little dipping his hand in the paint bothered him. He stuck his palm to the tree and grinned.

That night, Nan made her favorite spaghetti and meatballs, a meal Bailey hadn't seen in ages. They ate together for the first time in a long while, and Nan gave Mia platefuls of seconds and thirds, always seeming to forget she'd just gotten more.

"So, where are you from?" Nan asked through a mouth of ground beef and spaghetti.

"Tri State area," Mia replied, curling a crude amount of noodles around her fork.

"That's a long way away."

Mia shrugged.

"And your mamma's got a new boyfriend?"

"Yeah," said Mia. "He's dull but he's all right."

"And your mamma? What's she like?"

"Nan, stop prying," Bailey said, his eyes darting to Mia. She

21

had already lowered her fork.

"What?" said Nan, scowling. "I'm just trying to get to know the girl."

"Mean," Mia said. "She's mean."

"Let me get you another helping." Nan snatched her plate and hobbled to the stove.

Mia looked to Nan and then to Bailey, her brow pulling together.

"So how about it?" Bailey said, eager for a change of subject. "Can we stay in the tent tonight?"

Nan placed her plate in the sink and flicked on the faucet. "I guess it'll be fine," she said. "But don't you stay up too late."

Bailey beamed at Mia. It took Mia a moment before she smiled back, and even then she didn't look him in the eye, but Bailey knew if they could just get out to the tent, play some games and eat peanuts from tin cans, it'd be all right. Mia would know Nan was harmless, just old and indelicate. She'd know that once they got out to the tent.

Mia was quiet the rest of supper, and she was quiet while they scrubbed the dishes.

"I'm gonna go grab some overnight stuff," she said to him once they'd cleared the table. "From Jim's, you know."

Bailey looked at her. "But don't you have your backpack with you?"

Her jaw set as she smacked the faucet off. "I own other things."

"Yeah, of course," Bailey said, nodding. "I'll meet you out there in fifteen minutes, OK?"

She looked at him for a moment before turning her head. "See you later," she said.

"Fifteen minutes?" He felt for the braid of grass in his pocket. Nothing.

In one quick swipe, Mia peeled off a bandage and stuck it to Bailey's forehead. She smirked, and Bailey's mouth popped open, and then they were smiling. Bailey noticed then that she had a freckle in her left iris. It was the first time he'd been so close to her eyes. But then her smirk shifted into something empty, not even sad but almost gone altogether, and she agreed, "Fifteen minutes."

The next day Bailey looked out the kitchen window, staring at the padded-down square of grass just beyond the backyard gate. He hadn't slept, waiting for Mia all night, venturing to the fence in pitch darkness, the pond in restful morning sun. But she was gone. Their bungalow had been dismantled and tucked away, the encyclopedias returned to their shelves, the Band-Aid boxes marinated in the garbage pail. Nothing was left except the ghost of the tent's weight, the grass pressed into a smooth square.

When Nan's jar of starter began bubbling over, Bailey reached for a towel and sprayed his bottle of cleanser, watching it plume into foam on the countertop. His eyes burned as he scrubbed back and forth, unaware that one day he'd forget Mia's face, her crooked body, her quick and hulking laugh. One day, he'd only remember her blue and green Band-Aids.

WHEN YOU TELL ME YOUR FATHER CAME BACK

in the form of a bird, I say my mother knows
I tolerated her. Sometimes even liked her.
Especially when she laid aside her pain

massaging almost reverently its furrows,
at the foot of her bed and told the old stories.
I cannot say now whether she is Appaloosa

or Paint, or one of the old dogs in the grain
but the smell of hay, and the way sun fingers
dust-motes of summers in the barn loft

softens me like yesterday's child.
Sometimes poems come with the body,
intact. Sometimes they,

like I do, shapeshift, shake out feathers,
fly against the wind. She tells me
my father arose, having shed death, in search

of his voice. He could never bear her
being away too long, though in the end it was he
left her for his mistress, leukemia. Seven years

gone now. It was on some path toward Hurricane Ridge
Mom and I saw the raven in wind-stunted trees,
calling for his mate. From her wheelchair

Mom hissed it away, but raven stayed.
I silently prayed to it, saying to it *Father,*
here is my mother.

20 WEEKS: IMAGINING

And still I wait to lift your body I imagine it
long enough to survive until I imagine it

again you twitching under my wife's skin
shuddering in her abdomen against her ribs

you want out of the universe that keeps you
alive already I am scared you will be

another one of us falling out of love with ourselves
and a little too curious about nothingness

they have shown us your image like chalk
carved in obsidian half-dark on the ultrasound

mouth open for your first hungry breaths of amnios
I have seen you vanish into visible sound

layers of tissue returning like water filling holes
on the beach it is the way of the earth to bury us

I am not your father yet so I can say this
without fear of failure someone should tell you

about pillows about pineapples someone should
tell you about jackhammers and tap water

in Florida about sneezing someone should remind you
about the way we saw you first a pebble in ocean

anything could have carried you away afterward
we walked it was winter we shuffled over the ice

A few blocks from here Amee had seen four trains
running at the same time, but she only knew one kind
that stopped – the one with the animals.

PURPLE SKY

Wednesday nights the flies came. Wiggled through the old screens, knocked drunkenly around the kitchen, settled on the trashcan overloaded with diapers and dinner scraps. Wails came from the train yard like the air was haunted. Amee stood by the small stove light batting flies and eating cheese as she cut it. The windows were dark. She saw the streetlight but not the men. The basketball hit the drive, rim, backdrop, puncturing the ghostly moans. She and Joe moved to the neighborhood two months ago, the same week as William moved here with his story worse than theirs. He provided escape from diaper loads, milk stains, scrubbed fingernails, piercing squawks in the dead of night—an infant was an animal. William had eyed her and Joe slumped on the couch like he knew who they'd be in ten years: ironic, divorced, twenty pounds overweight.

Nine minutes since Laurelee cried. Easier to think of her sweet pink face without the panic that came calming her because the doctor said babies sense stress, looking at Amee while he said it, and now she didn't let the baby see her face when she cried. Which Joe said was crazy but what could she do? She couldn't change her face. Her own mother had propped bottles against pillows; sores had spread across Amee's mouth for a week before her mother had gotten the infection treated. A litany of sins her mom admitted after she'd had Lauralee; she several times drank wine with friends down the hall and came back hours later to Amee shrieking "like a burned rat." Parents were given babies like pets; there were no tests, no practice; anyone with ten months to spare was allowed to bring one home.

The ball's beats slowed then ceased. Only the moaning remained: big, dumb animals being tortured; the flies came with the half-dead cows on that train that stopped here overnight for some reason. Amee cut up an orange thinking she'd leave half for Joe then sat at the table and ate his pieces slowly. The first couple weeks she'd invited William inside but he didn't know when to leave and she didn't like to be known as a bitch. She and Joe named the driveway the limit.

The screen door opened and Joe said, "Sky's purple. Come see."

"He still out there?"

"Yep."

She didn't worry about Joe here. He didn't drink or lock himself in rooms. He was from this small Nebraska town, had lived with his parents and brothers in this house that had been cemented to the ground for a hundred and forty years, on this street with no sirens or glass breaking, no people screaming at each other, no gunshots. The women who'd lived here and gave birth here: Amee sometimes imagined she was them, walking from room to room while Joe went interviewing. The house was big enough that those early women must've been rich, with husbands who owned half the town in crops or were investors who thought why wouldn't people want to live in the middle of nowhere Nebraska?

Joe thought she minded but she didn't. In some part of her brain lay things she cared about besides the house and baby — she'd planned to get a doctorate, conduct studies, own mice — but they wouldn't come into focus. She needed a microscope, a scientific manual. Someday she'd tweeze out old ambitions and trap them between glass, slide them under a light, or else serenely lose them in the cracks.

She followed Joe outside. William sat on the lawn leaning with his elbow on one knee, his big shoulders uneven. Why he'd moved to this neighborhood of paint-peeled houses and popped-up weeds, all shedding and blemishes—he'd come from the west-side mansions—she didn't know. He wore a T-shirt and basketball shorts. He must have come home and put these things on and waited for Joe to take out the trash. It was too dark to see his face.

"We'll hear her," Joe told Amee, sitting by William. "Have to come out this far."

Amee stayed on the porch. She saw where they were looking. "It's the lights from the amphitheater." She'd read about it opening this weekend with a local country band. Now that she was listening, she heard the human crooning alongside the animal moans.

"The sky's full of bruises," William said. He had a potbelly bigger than the basketball. He had two teenage kids. "It's a punch in the stomach."

"The place I told Amee about isn't here anymore," Joe said. "You could hear the corn grow."

"Corn doesn't grow now," William said. "It shoots from the ground like bullets, more machine than plant."

A train whistled and roared for a long minute like music from another dimension. Its alien whine, its layers of echoes, obliterated all other crooning.

"I like the trains here," Amee said. "They rock me to sleep."

"Trains shake loose the houses," William said. "It's why the paint peels."

"Of course trains don't soothe the baby," Joe said. Last night Lauralee cried so hard and so long before she got the baby sling that Amee asked if Joe thought crying could kill her. The sobs sounded sometimes like choking.

"Babies don't like men," William told Joe. "Later she'll like you."

"Come on out, Amee," Joe said. "We'll hear her."

Amee leaned against the rail of the porch. "I've seen the sky lit before."

William glanced at Joe—she was being rude. Across the street ran ruptured rooflines and broken shingles she hadn't noticed when Joe first brought her here; "Sweet neighborhood," she'd said, still pregnant and dopey, not that she'd learned much since. If she was smart, she would be sleeping.

"It's a hundred years from now that I worry about." William spun the basketball in his hands. "These seeds coated with poison and the sun getting through holes. No stars, no quiet. It's fine for us but the kids should have better."

"They won't know a difference," Joe said.

"That's the problem with getting old. Knowing things. Better to stay dumb, Amee." He looked at her. "Don't pay attention to anything out here."

"I'm not dumb," she said. Joe looked at her, too.

"I meant it as a compliment," William said.

The amphitheater crooning stopped. The animals moaned on, less steady in volume and pitch, but deeper, sadder. She did feel like a child again. There was a bubble, only different things were inside it this time.

A red light flickered on the street: a high school kid on his bike. He wore a black sweatshirt and dark jeans and carried a backpack. Some parent let this kid leave the house blending into night; of course Amee's mother had barely noticed what she wore either.

He stopped in their driveway. "I brought milk." He dropped his backpack off his shoulder.

"I have milk," William told him. "It's not dementia. One time I forgot."

"Mom said to bring it."

William bounced the ball to Joe. "We'll scrounge something." The boy followed William across the street and his white sneakers sparked the pavement so sadness cracked in Amee. She wanted to close her eyes and see a different picture. Joe stayed on the grass, passing the ball between his hands. A porch light came on down the street spotlighting a rounded red door. It looked like it led to a fairytale.

"He's giving me a job," Joe said. "Admin assistant."

"Does he pay in world-weary platitudes? We could use more of those in our bank account."

"We'll find you a job next. Make friends. If it doesn't work, we'll move back to Omaha."

"I'm attached to this house. Don't you see it growing on my hip? It's not a complaint. My hips were never going to stay the same size."

Another train whistled, obscuring the wails again. Eight tracks through this town. A few blocks from here Amee had seen four trains running at the same time, but she only knew one kind that stopped — the one with the animals.

Joe leaned on the rail beside her. A cool breeze blew. "Last chance to see the purple sky."

"It isn't the last time. It isn't going back to black."

He nudged her waist with his hip. "One day when the whole sky's purple we'll say remember when it started? We lived in Nebraska."

A wail carried from the house. Rose in pitch, broke, repeated: the baby drowned out the train, the cows. Joe looked up like the porch roof was what cried. They went into the pocked-wood entryway where warm air hung. Her old textbooks — Chemistry, Shakespeare, The History of the Civilized World — covered a stretch of exposed ductwork.

"Get ready for a long night." Amee pulled the sling's straps over her shoulders; they fit grooves in her skin.

"Let me tonight." Joe held the basketball in the crook of his arm.

"Next time." The sling felt light. The baby's cries crescendoed. Flies sprang from the stairs with each step. At first she'd wondered if she alone could hear the ghost train's lonely wails, but no: Joe told her they were cows, on their way to slaughter. Not lonely but scared, having spent their whole life in one small stall that stayed still only to be forced in this other small stall that moved and stopped and those cows wondering when it would move again.

In the dark room, the baby's cries drowned out the town. Amee's body tensed but her chest ached for the sobs and shakes that would fall against it, the primitive metronome of a second heartbeat. She turned her face from her baby and listened.

SOLASTALGIA

Solastalgia: the distress caused
by environmental change
                    —Glenn Albrecht, Ph.D.

The small town seemed smaller
when I finally returned — the mountains,
the airport,   the two-lane highway,
   even my mother's shoulders
as she gave me a welcome home hug.

Every place in my memory   was gone.
My grade school,   my high school,
the town's lone, vintage gas pump,
and the tiny, square hot dog stand,   once
the social hub   of the community.

What hadn't been destroyed   by fire, flood,
storms, and chemical spills,   had withered
away   and disappeared   as disasters
and death   drove droves away —
a mass exodus   of Appalachians.

I sailed around the world   only to find
that I am now the one   left behind,
without an anchor,   haunted
  and homesick   for a home
that no longer exists.

FOOD DESERTS OF MEMPHIS

in August on the death anniversary
of a king or prophet of gyrations
          a generation once attempted
          to mimic like chants said
with hips rather than mouths
heat and humidity melts skin
          no one can tell
          the difference between tears
and sweat even as pilgrims
hold votive candles to their faces
          Memphis filled with homes
          Graceland the only famous one
others owned by working class
searching couch cushions and pockets
          for snack cigarette gas money
          Memphis filled with pockets
of food deserts long mazes
of cracked and pockmarked asphalt
          you could get lost in on your way
          to find fresh meat eggs vegetables
pilgrimages if piggy banks
couches wallets are not filled
          enough for a tank of gas
          the wait for buses up to two hours
paths to grocery stores
up to four miles

sweat beads up onto skin
like condensation on beer
and water bottles
it sticks like puddles of mud
on the river bank from humidity
without it going into the air
where it should two hours
in the August sun can kill a man

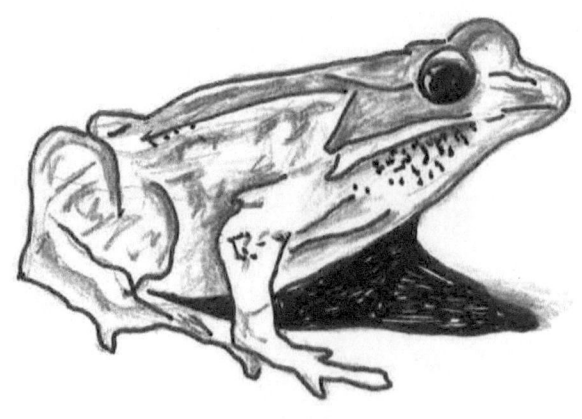

If I were a wood frog, I would avoid the kiss of princesses,
revel in mud baths, and bury myself until motionless.

DORMANCY

My older sister wakes me by playing the opening song from *The Lion King*, downloaded special for her visit to my home. "The Circle of Life" has been on her tablet for days, waiting for this moment. Really loud, R mimes the grandiose motion of a baboon wielding a lion cub at me. I remind her that women in their thirties get limited Disney references per day. She has used hers. This is patently untrue, but I was warm before she removed my comforter, and now I am cold. And anyway, I'm only just getting back to a normal sleeping pattern, the kind I don't have to lie about.

Canadian scientists test the freeze-thaw cycles of wood frogs, whose siblings don't wake them with any song humans know. Their rasping croaks are broken or loose instrument strings played over water. The kind of sound my violin made when the pegs unwound and the strings made a deep vibrating twang. These violin frogs still their vocal cords and bury themselves alive in winter, a natural preservation instinct, and their bodies freeze, entering what National Geographic calls "a state of suspended animation."

If I were a wood frog, I would avoid the kiss of princesses, revel in mud baths, and bury myself until motionless.

I'm not a wood frog, so instead I say, "coffee" to my sister.

"No, no more coffee for you. Wakey wakey, eggs and bakey," she says.

"Coffee. Make me coffee."

"Don't know how. Wouldn't do it if I did."

I put in a request for more minutes.

"No more minutes," she says.

"Coffee."

"Coffee," she says, sad. "This is no kind of life for you."

She retreats and in another thirty minutes, I join her in the living room, where I still don't have coffee, and the room is still cold to conserve heat. I'm undeservedly cranky as it is almost noon.

But, until recently, I was spending from 3:00 AM to 4:00 PM in bed, shunning the hours in which I'm expected to complete tasks. To be an adult with email responses to write — don't forget the header and a professional closing. To take out the rotting mushrooms in my kitchen trash can rather than just lighting a "Northwoods Nights" candle near the bin. Oil changes and small talk. These are not difficult tasks individually, but together, they are a collection of infinite *I should be doing tasks*. I wouldn't call my avoidance depression, and laziness is just unflattering enough that I'm willing to seriously consider the state of dormancy described by the Unitarian minister at the rare service I attended on Christmas Eve.

"Even roses," the minister said. "Must go dormant in order to bloom." A woman waved her hands in a gesture of silent applause for the sentiment, pausing from her knitting project, what appeared to be a mitten, left or right unknown.

Roses — like bears, skunks, bats, bees, snakes, groundhogs — are more than shielded from the inhospitable weather of winter in their dormancy. Their dormancy, or hibernation, is time to gather strength. And maybe that is all I'm really looking for. A moment of dormancy that is about gathered strength rather than avoidance and protection.

Still, the possibility of strength gathered in dormancy is closed to humans with cats to feed and rent to pay. This doesn't stop me from imagining.

I once visited a wildlife center that specialized in rodents. There was a tunnel with windows to view the sleeping balls of nested fur. Weasels had their heads tucked around their bodies, their eyes covered by a hugging tail, and I wondered if early humans slept approximately the same number of hours per night as these rodents, if they slept when it became dark and cold and if civilization necessarily means ignoring instinct because we can. We are perpetually the rose trying to bud.

At the peak of my exhaustion, I told my mother, "I've learned I'm tired because I'm getting ready to *bloom*."

"The minister said that?" she asked.

My sister has settled onto the couch, and I don't feel particularly energized after "The Circle of Life," but if I drink enough caffeine, I will feel different than now. I will microwave yesterday's coffee, and it will be different than it was yesterday too. I plug in a light that is meant to dilate my eyes and simulate the sun, a remedy for Seasonal Affective Disorder. Don't look directly into the lightbox, the instructions remind. My cat, who doesn't read, makes himself into a loaf directly in front of the lightbox. I take my reuptake inhibitor, my vitamin D, and I avoid telling anyone about how tired I feel.

Wood frogs enter a state of dormancy deeper than sleep and feel no shame. They tuck limbs and allow ice to form beneath skin, snow to crystalize on their head. But global rises in temperature may be changing the natural freeze-thaw cycle of amphibians. To study this phenomenon, zoologists tested the *cryoprotectant* properties of North American wood frogs, capturing and inducing dormancy with increasing cold and eventual darkness. At the end of the study, scientists only collected data from the remaining live frogs. I'm not interested in their findings, only the increasingly sedate frogs being lulled to hibernation.

To avoid inducing further dormancy, I sip coffee and open the blinds to let in gray light. Bundled-up children play across the field. They wear puffed coats and hats. They are supposed to play with the goal posts, chase the soccer ball across the frosted grass.

There is also a kickball game in progress, but a small group of puffs are in the outfield grass, immobile in the field, waiting for the bell to ring. Winter in the Pacific Northwest is not cold in the way my childhood home in Wisconsin was, but living here can be a bit like water torture, slow, cold dripping over a restrained forehead. The drips hitting a jumping vein between eyebrows to roll over the nose, cheek, mouth. Everyone seems to be deliberating on what isn't so bad about the weather. Comparisons are made.

I can't resist comparing this rain to the snow and ice of my childhood. The way we went skating on a small pond in the middle of the woods. My "skates" were metal platforms strapped to the soles of my boots, each skate had two blades to help me balance the considerable weight and bulk of snowpants and a parka. I don't remember who was with me. I remember looking down through the frozen pond to see the outlines of immobile frogs, frozen mid-leap, bubbles stopped. Now, I know large numbers of frogs are a sign of a healthy ecosystem. Then, I didn't know about "indicator species." I was uncertain of the life cycle of frogs, but I wondered if they would thaw in spring, continue on to finish whatever they meant to do.

The apartment warms slowly after I turn the heat back on. On my couch, two blankets are tucked around my sister like restraints. Her hands are cold. Someone told her that cold hands were considered an attractive feminine trait during an earlier time, but she just looks cold, and I can't see her face under her hood. The rest of her is frequently cold also. The adrenaline of waking me has passed, and she is especially chilly now, wearing fuzzy pink and purple unicorn pants, a thick sweatshirt.

I sit on the floor, leaning against the couch. I'm wearing a short-sleeved t-shirt that says, "I work hard so my cat can have a better life."

From beneath the unicorns and fleece, she repeats: "I'm cold. I'm cold. I'm cold." A mantra which is followed by a shivering sound that has enough flourish it is made plural and comes out sounding something like: *Burrrsies.*

"Mom hates when I say that," she says.

"I wonder why," I say. I know why.

I imagine her reporting on her bodily temperature each morning as she has done this morning. It is her version of morning coffee, a ritual to get the day started.

Sometimes, I, too, catch myself in a ritual of coldness I learned to do as a child. I use my index finger to press the end of my nose into the indentation or philtrum, above my upper lip, a perfect fit if I stretch my upper lip up at the same time I push my nose down. Someone once told me touching my hands to my neck, lips, cheeks, or nose is an unconscious self-soothing technique. Newborns, this person claimed, do this instinctually. The same person told me, don't touch your hair or shoulder during a job interview. It shows anxiety, weakness. When I hear this, I want to have a tail and to curl it around myself, to have the ability to freeze myself, to have time to rest but also time to gather myself.

Instinctively, we touch our faces an average of about 16 times per hour according to The U.S National Library of Medicine. Do we have that many itches? Is our hair in constant need of adjustment? On some unconscious level, are we soothed by the feel of human touch, even, or especially, our own? A reassuring reminder, I am in my body. I can spread warmth through the nerve endings in my lips with my own fingertips. I suspect this is why wood frogs lie upon their own limbs in dormancy, even if they can't feel their own heart beating, they still want to.

"I'm cold. Cold. Cold," she is still saying.

I inhale coffee. The stale liquid reminds me of old cigarettes and ritualistic early morning balcony smokers.

"Are you cold?" I ask.

Before my sister visited, over the holiday break, I stayed in bed for longer and longer, the blankets piled on top of me, a physical weight to press organs together. If I kept my eyes closed and my mind blank, I could fall into a half-sleep. Still aware of my body, I would dream of ladders going up and up, curling staircases, infinite doors. Each time I selected a door, staircase, ladder, the dream revealed another set of options. I burrowed into a nest of blankets each night in anticipation of the dreams. One sheet, one comforter, two couch throw blankets, and a pillow to give weight to the body beneath. My back became sore, dehydration in my kidneys and a full bladder, accompanying a thirteen-hour sleep. The soreness penetrated sleep, making my body real, in dreams too. These dreams only came after oversleeping, in the twelfth, thirteenth, and fourteenth hour. At least, I only remembered them when I'd overslept, and being able to carry the feeling of height and choice into the daytime was the point.

During the day, choices feel limited, and I've never done quite enough work. There will always be lessons to plan, meals to prepare, prescriptions to pick up, fridges to clean, floors that could be vacuumed. Each task becomes a commentary on the success or failure of the day. Did I complete the maximum number of possible tasks, and did I do so without poppy seeds in my teeth? I check and recheck my teeth before leaving a room, tell myself, stand more naturally — *no, naturally* — do something with my hand. This is a kind of anxiety that no amount of breathing exercises or thought record charts will alleviate, a constantly exhausting task. Sometimes it is easier to just give in to the worry of direct or implied critiques, even if they are my own.

I'm always making observations about the status of my bodies in order to change the status of my body, but what is the difference between contentment and stasis? Contentment is stability and ease. Stasis is a condition I associate with depression and the questions my doctor asks. In my den of blankets, which am I experiencing? Maladaptive depression or just a natural state of dormancy. Most of the time, I missed most of the daylight hours. There was no point in showering or getting dressed. I made goals for myself and tried to be awake on weekends, but I am so tired.

Depression categorizes sleep as a symptom, but it doesn't need to be. Can I choose to be in bed and is the act of deciding the difference between health and illness? There is no one normal or average, only ideas about what I *should* do, and I'm prone to seeing footage of grizzly bears getting ready to rest and asking questions they don't ask themselves. What has made that bear sad?

With half a cup of coffee left, I tell my sister to shower.

"We don't have to go. What do you think? Do you want to?"

"You decide," I say.

We are going to look for seals today. My sister is visiting from Wisconsin, and we must have adventures to record. If we ever start the day, get off the couch and floor, shower, etc. I want to show her the sea stars too, but we question if the conditions for sea stars are right. Contrary to their name, do they gravitate to the surface only during sunnier weather?

She is still very cold, she reminds me, and it is my turn to shower first.

I would never leave the house if I didn't have to, or maybe I would, given six months to get ready. I once read that a bear in hibernation will not wake even if there is a loud noise. Such is the assertiveness of their biological drive to sleep. I imagine myself capable of flight and assertiveness after a six-month sleep, but I will always lack the drive to stay asleep through the noise. This won't stop me from trying.

During dormancy, the heart of a wood frog doesn't beat, and there is no nerve or brain activity to report the frog's body to itself. I imagine myself giving in to the exhaustion like a wood frog, tucking my limbs beneath my curled body, my heart slowing, stopping. Feeling would cease in each fingertip until my brain stopped articulating the lack of blood flow and the need to schedule an eye exam, call for new insurance cards, make the payment. I am not a wood frog. I can feel the heat vent kicking on. I can smell my own body. I get off the couch, shower, dress, put on shoes, and all the while my sister looks out the window as rain becomes sleet. We could stay in, I think, wrap ourselves in fleece and dim the lights like Alaskan wood frogs who sometimes thaw themselves too soon, false springs in late winter.

PROCESSION

Driving to work Good Friday, I saw the cross
    borne by children and all day carried the sight of this ancient

procession. That was the intent of the priest leading them, I suppose,
    as if this anachronism — the priest's long robes, the heavy

cross shouldered by children in modern dress,
    attempting solemnity, lamenting down a busy street

could unsettle us all from complacency in this world.
    All we who are skeptical of salvation.

It seems as though we've had nothing but rain since then
    and front doors are swelling so that neighbors are having

to find other ways in and out of their homes
    but at this moment the sky is blue and I hear

the soft autumn chatter of the birds and squirrels.
    Just a few leaves have changed color.

I watch one drift down. The sun warms my hands.

CUANDO LLUEVE

Te dejé junto al ocote que sembramos
a la orilla del río
el día en que desabotonamos el fuego
y lo fundimos en abraso,
en el adiós me diste el ítacate de tus besos
y salí del pueblo con una calma en los huaraches
se quedó atrás el cerro, el río y la Malintzi,
el aroma del campo cuando llueve
y los ocotes.
Ahora,
con la piel ultrajada
y sin brillo en los ojos,
regreso lentamente,
paso a paso,
al ocote en que olvidé tu cabellera.

WHEN IT RAINS

I left you next to the ocote tree we sowed
by the river
the day we unbuttoned the fire
and melted it in an ember,
in the goodbye you gave me the food of your kisses
and I left the village in calm in my sandals
the hill, the river, and the Malinche volcano stayed behind,
the smell of the earth when it rains
and the ocote trees.
Now,
with outraged skin
and no shine in my eyes,
I come back slowly,
step by step,
to the ocote tree where I forgot your hair.

translated by Toshiya Kamei

JARDÍN DE SOMBRAS

Tus pies descalzos en la vereda
son hojas sueltas,
pensamientos que tocan el barro
y comienzan a danzar sobre humedad.
Un aroma a tierra mojada se desprende del pirul,
llega a mi memoria como la sombra de los manzanos.
Eres ondulación justa en umbral de la música que surge de mi
    vientre,
eres ave,
pájaro azul de hoja en flor;
cantas tu desnudez con el pincel
y levantas las ramas del olvido con tus labios.
Trinas alegre a los ciruelos
cuando nacen sus flores a lo lejos
en una tinta china.

La luna, en su absoluta elegancia de equinoccio,
ilumina tus pasos
a cada golpe de pincel;
nace una sombra que danza
ensimismada sobre la tela.

GARDEN OF SHADOWS

Your bare feet on the sidewalk
are loose leaves,
thoughts that touch the mud
and start dancing on humidity.
A scent of wet earth emerges from the pepper tree,
and reaches my memory like the shadow of apple trees.
You're a ripple on the threshold of the music sprouting from
   my womb.
You're a bird,
a blue bird with leaf in flower;
You sing your nudity with the brush
and lift the branches of oblivion with your lips.
You chirp cheerfully to plums
when their flowers are born in the distance
in a Chinese ink.

The moon, in its absolute elegance of equinox,
illuminates your steps
in each brush stroke;
a shadow that dances is born,
self-absorbed on the cloth.

translated by Toshiya Kamei

*I've received boxes of Lucky Charms for joke birthday
presents, and I've been kissed by random strangers
on St. Patty's Day.*

PO-TAY-TO/PO-TAH-TO

I pick up a white box with colorful imagery of DNA. The middle of the box reads,

Welcome to you.

Had I never met me?

A family member gave me the kit as a gift, and I couldn't help but think I was entering into some kind of spit-collecting pyramid scheme. After a person buys a kit, 23andMe tries to sell that consumer additional kits at discount.

"Buy 23andMe for the entire family and discover more connections."

Connections for me meant talking some distant relative in the middle of Europe into letting me crash on their sofa for free. At least, that's what 23andMe commercials promise. My long-lost distant cousin might have a mustache or a funny hat, but we'll hug with the affection only two people who share chromosomes can feel.

Inside the box is a plastic tube for saliva. I search the 23andMe website to register my mouth juices, and I find out the profile will include, among other things, ethnicity percentages, and ancestral matches. On the 23andMe homepage, a picture of a young woman appears with a long chart of multiple ethnicities and a variety of percentages next to her face. Her skin is light brown with freckles scattered across her skinny nose. Her dark hair is styled in an Afro, and her green eyes shine like translucent pigment in blown glass. I think to myself, *maybe I am just as genetically interesting as her.*

Is it a strange thing to be genetically jealous? To want to have what someone else has, chromosomally speaking? Is being genetically jealous simply what I feel when I wish to have wavy hair, or at least to be someone not so pale, white-skinned, redheaded, brown-eyed, with an average height and skinny body type and a last name so synonymous with Irish descent that my mind feels like a dumpster of jokes about being Irish from other people laid at me in the hope that I might fake an Irish accent for them or dance a jig when I'm drunk.

Can I buy you a Guinness?

People have given me Irish flags, four-leaf clover keychains, leprechaun shirts, and journals with Celtic knot imprints. I've received boxes of Lucky Charms for joke birthday presents, and I've been kissed by random strangers on St. Patty's Day. I have been asked multiple times if I get mean when I drink, and I've dated a woman whose mom warned her about Irish temperament, poverty, and alcoholism.

Maybe genetic jealousy creates the same desire that puts a fake indigenous princess in a family book without thought of the historical bullshit of doing such a thing. I remember my dad believed he had "Indian blood" because he liked to go camping and walk barefoot.

When my Irish-ness is brought up through jest or by glances after James Joyce is referenced, I would be nice to say with some authority that "I'm not *just* Irish."

I get on the 23andMe website a few days later, and I still haven't registered. Even though I want to prove myself as something else besides Irish, I'm hesitant to give my spit to them along with the implicit power to infer Me from DNA.

This time on the website, a white woman with long straight blonde hair and a bulbous nose smiles towards some text. She's wearing a sweater and a beanie.

Everyone has a DNA story. What is your story? [shop now]

Behind her is a number.

"Scandinavian 34.5%"

How is a percentage a story?

Here's another percentage: 99.9% of your DNA is similar to everyone else. But of course, it's the promise of meaning from that .1% difference between us that people pay to have their DNA sequenced. Even with all our genetics codified, categorized, compared, analyzed, and represented, doesn't the story of me come after my genes are interpreted, not before?

I once stayed with this embodiment of ancestral storytelling, and he might agree that genetics equate to story. He was a friend of a friend, and had offered us lodging while we explored New York City. He had a large red beard with red hair trimmed short and monkish. He was six-foot-five, and his body was a series of rounded hills of muscle.

"Another red head," he said to me with a booming voice when we met. He shook my hand and squeezed it hard. "I bet everyone thinks you're Irish, huh?"

I've probably used this same line with others who carry two recessive allele copies on their number 16 chromosome.

"I'm a Viking," he said, unprompted. "My family is from Denmark. Some great-ancestor way back." He thumbed over his shoulder into history. He wore a sleeveless shirt, and on one bicep was a tattoo with Nordic letters wrapped around his arm.

He asked me where my red hair was from. To avoid the heritage-games, I told him I didn't know. His eyes ran up and down my comparatively scrawny body.

"What's your last name?"

"Kelley."

A knowing smile spread across his lips. "Irish!"

At night we laid in separate beds four-feet across from one another. Before he turned out the light, he showed me a poster of his family crest on the wall. Family crests not side-by-side always look the same to me. Do they always have a castle?

If I had a family crest of the ancestors I truly know, it would include a can of Budweiser, a Mormon beehive with a cloaked figure sneaking inside, a belt, and to represent just how Irish my family is, in my mind — that damn box of Lucky Charms. Under the icons would be the family motto: *Don't be a fool, wrap your tool.*

"Are you dating anyone?" Mr. Viking asked from the dark.

"I'm not," I said. The silence hung a bit uncomfortable, like he was expecting me to elaborate. I waited, and then asked if he were in a relationship.

"A gorgeous redhead," he said. He showed me a picture of her from his phone. "I would love to have redheaded kids," he said. "Wouldn't you?"

"I haven't thought much about kids, or their hair. I guess it would be nice to stand next to another redhead from my family so that when strangers ask if we're related that it would finally be true."

I told him about a woman with red hair I often went out with. Every time we were asked, we made up fake family histories.

We only found out we had the same father a week ago.

We're twins. Can't you tell?

We're cousins, but we grew up in the same house because our parents thought all of the redheads should live together.

Mr. Viking chuckled. "Random people ask my girlfriend and I all the time if she's my sister. I think people wonder, until they see us hold hands or kiss."

"Or maybe they still wonder," I said.

We laughed, and when we went quiet and I was ready to be done with the night, he said, "I think it's best to stick to your type, you know?"

"Like hair color?" I playfully asked, thinking he was about to go off about personality or astrology.

"Even if she wasn't a redhead I'd still date her because she's of Scandinavian descent, like me."

I stopped laughing. Clearly hair color or personality was not what he meant by *type*.

"I'm not a racist," he said. "I'm just proud of my heritage. I feel like people of the same heritage belong to one another. It keeps their own culture alive. If people just end up with whoever from wherever, it actually makes the world less diverse because all these heritages get lost in the mixing."

I let the remark hover in the dark and remain unanswered. This was a mistake, and I felt it while I waited for the morning. I like to think that if I had been older, I would have challenged him by using Socratic digging to take out the seeds of a racist logic from his mind. Now, nearly ten years later, I wonder what became of him as his worldview plays out in places like Charlottesville where white marchers chanted, "You will not replace us" — a reference to their pseudo-sociological belief that they are under threat of cultural genocide.

If Mr. Viking is single today, he's in luck. Dating services and forums have already popped up based on genetic testing. He would have to decide if someone like the model with 34.5% Scandinavian DNA was enough for him, or if he needed to see her other ratios to make a final decision to ask her out on a date. If he had the chance, would he have asked his girlfriend to get her DNA sequenced?

I love you, but, I just want to make sure.

The 23andMe kit was given to me as a gift, but giving my genetic information to a company worries me. Some days when I think about all that Google and Facebook have on me, I feel like I'm one targeted advertisement away from moving to an offline shack in the Idaho mountains. Genetic advertisers that know my potential for health conditions and diseases could market wonder pills, health programs, or sunscreen to me that sound scientifically curated. If these advertisers know my heritage, they might even try to send ads of Irish paraphernalia and decorations.

The world wants to define us, or at least to have us select a pre-fab definition. When we are defined and when we believe in that definition, we can be marketed to by corporations, political groups, and by potential sexual partners. The more we fit into a category, and the more people can be moved into a category, the more effective and efficient those marketers become.

And being defined, genetically, also makes the horrors of eugenics, nationalism, and ethnic persecution or disenfranchisement easier, especially if our information is available and searchable. The more our bodies become digitized knowledge, the more we are at risk for being targeted for nefarious reasons. There are reasons beyond privacy for why I did not want to have my genes sequenced. I don't always want to know my ancestry. Ancestry can be confused with fate and the mere knowledge of being from a particular lineage could subconsciously play on how I see myself or my family. But genetic knowledge might also challenge a false heritage that an identity is based on. Red hair and freckly skin are not just phenotypes of genes that are passed down from Celtics or even Western Europeans. My hair and skin could be from an original genetic mutation, one that can occur in any ethnicity. There are African redheads, Polynesian redheads, and redheads from South America and Asia.

In 23andMe advertisements, people find out they have ancestral DNA that makes them seek out and learn more about those other ethnicities. This is the hope—that knowledge of our ancestry makes us respect human diversity and history more. The chances of someone being purely of one ethnicity, or even of a group of ethnicities that are associated with a color of skin, is so slight, that it rocks the myths of race for people like Mr. Viking.

I'm only 34.5% Scandinavian? Fuck.

And not all Scandinavians were Vikings.

Americans can be historically naïve, and genetic testing could positively challenge our personal histories and national consciousness. Let the past be the past, some say, but this might be impossible to mutter with a weightless heart after a genetic test links someone to a perpetrator of a historical injustice.

In one of the many family stories that I distrust, my racist grandfather told me that someone in our direct family line owned a slave plantation in Nashville that was burned down during the Civil War. There are no records or evidence, supposedly, because the courthouse that stored them was also burned by Union soldiers. Does the story mean I have a duty to find out the facts? How much burden would I face because of my lineage, if it is true? Would the 23andMe test even be able to shed light on this time in my ancestral history, or would it continue to be an undocumented gap?

I could throw these questions away and not hold myself responsible for what my ancestors might have done, but I also shouldn't need a genetic test to accept and reckon with the truth that those of white heritage have benefited more from their white skin than others have from their darker skins. I don't know if a genetic test will reveal just how many racists and how deep the racism runs in my ancestry, but it does terrify me a bit to know for certain with the ancestral tools being developed by 23andMe that could show that I'm the direct descendent of a slave owner.

My grandpa told the story with pride, and all I had was disgust. Maybe I should be equally disgusted with myself that in the back of my mind, I have a desire to disbelieve it without any counterevidence.

In the morning, I open up the 23andMe box and remind myself of an old saying: You shouldn't look a gift horse in the mouth. At the bathroom mirror, I push my red hair across my pale forehead and I wonder to what ends, if any, I will use the results.

I take out the spit tube, and fill it up.

DREAM IN WHICH OPRAH
SPEAKS TO MY MOTHER

The nurses told my mother she was ungrateful
to mourn her dead baby when she still had
one in a bundle. They said, do you know how
many mothers go home alone? I used to tell
her I remembered being born, and it always
made her laugh. She even told her friends, and
they laughed the sporadic, full laugh of not doing
dishes or laundry. They laughed the lie of being
happy. The doctors told her how lucky. My father
shuffled all things twin to thrift like cards or
shoes, took all the blue things back without receipt.

It is raining and I am watching Oprah
talk about grieving dead babies, miscarriages too.
Everything in my ground-level apartment
borrowed or shared. I call my mother to ask
her if she had my brother's footprints, anything
at all. She says she never even saw him
or held what was left, says that she was too lucky.
I never got rid of the reflex of falling. I start and fall
from my lover's arms, from the floor. What did I know?
I could only make an omelet at the stove. Oprah's
hands are folded on her lap, glamorous as silk napkins.

She takes my mother's hands in hers, one mother to the next
and says, Remember. Remembering is part of forgetting.

POMPEII

Tectonic plates colliding,
bass explodes like lava —
Ecstasy under Tempe skies.
Your lightning-yellow v-neck is

bass imploding like lava,
a florist gifting broken stems.
Your lightning-yellow v-neck is
still in my closet.

The florist gifted broken stems,
daisies you gave me each morning.
Your skeleton is still in my closet
dancing the mournful kung fu.

The daisies you gave me
my mother's favorite —
They dance the mournful kung fu
alone with cows in the pasture.

My mother's favorite
ecstasies, under small-town skies,
bow alone with bulls in the pasture,
their tectonic bass-lines colliding.

GIFT

When they find it, a grapefruit. The part of a woman's body
desired most, they check last. They use the word remission
not cure, a bridesmaid without a promise. You tell
me to name gratefulness for each insomnia: daughter,
dead mother, stillborn twin, even Grandmother Ruth,
your name a hand-me-down, gone at thirty-eight:
shoes, mittens, certain friends. When I run out I am
shocked or asleep. I write a crown of sonnets interrupted
for a lover no longer my lover, then your second surgery:
clean water, leaky roof, canned green-beans. You call me
to say six months. You say don't come, you are preparing.

I am grateful for the lover, no longer, the first I've named her
aloud in months. You last two. At the funeral I recite Milosz,
then I embarrass your father with a Christmas story
even though it is closer to Halloween. We are late
for the service because of your period and eye-shadow;
grateful for your fishnet stockings and miniskirt. The sanctuary
smells of pine garlands, the pastor telling the epic of birth.
I am thinking of Easter already, but all eyes are on you,
your stilettoed procession to the front pew. You are my idol
of idols. I know nothing of words or women, not yet.
When you sit, splinters snag your skirt.

SUCCESSION

And it starts with wheat going gray;
before long the whole field flattens,
rain hardens, whitens; rust settles in
for a long dark season. At night bird
after bird absconds with the burning
switchgrass. Surfaces turn unstable.
The heavying heads of scarecrows
bow to whatever gods grandfathers
believed in before giving up their
shirts and hats and faces to protect
the harvest. Note our autumn fury
already ash. Yesterday has left little
of itself untilled, and the *now* owns
nothing. It is time to crawl back into
our hands, asking what it is we have
done to deserve a fire that will last
until April. Starlight splays x-rays
of a leafless red oak against the red
side of an empty barn. Shovels snap
beneath our weight. Tinny voices of
old men talking about old men who
once spoke of flame and grace fade
slowly to static. This inherited story
slowly becomes our story. A wide-
open mouth somehow opens wider.

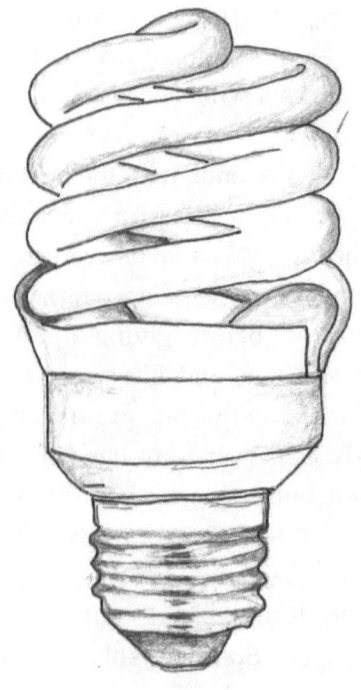

I hold out a compact fluorescent on the flat of my hand,
the way you offer food to a dog you don't know.

LET YOUR LIGHT SO SHINE

I point to the reflective gold letters spelling No Soliciting stuck on the metal screen door.

"We're not selling anything," Mrs. Fellows says. "We're *giving* them something." She motions me to knock. I tap on the rattling metal, which is cold even though the spring day is warm. It's an especially fancy screen door with a peacock tail pattern on the bottom half. "They won't hear a tap like that, Misty. You got to open the screen and *knock*."

Mrs. Fellows believes that using doorbells is "low class," and "loud enough to wake the dead. Civilized people knock." But she makes me do the actual knocking. To me, just opening the screen seems like intruding into the house. But I do it, rapping my knuckles against the dark finish of the front door, and wishing, for the billionth time, that I hadn't gotten stuck with Mrs. Fellows today. OK, so she's not really ancient, like Mrs. Peterson, who farts at coffee hour and pretends no one hears, or Mr. Devlin, who is always touching my arm or shoulder with his damp hand, like it's OK to paw me because I'm 14 and he's practically 100. But Mrs. Fellows is still old, old enough not to have a waist and to wear green eye shadow like it's stylish.

I wanted to pair up with Mr. Brian, the church's youth group leader. All the girls in the youth group have a crush on him. Even me, though I'm not stupid about it. I don't stay after Sunday school, inventing questions to ask him about the Bible lesson, or hike my skirt up to show my knees when I sit for class. No, when he puts his hand on my shoulder and leans down to check my answers in my workbook, I know he doesn't mean anything by it.

If I think about it later, that's my business. If I imagine the two of us walking through green hills spotted with orange poppies, the soft spring sun lighting his hair before he kisses me, I know it's just a fantasy. Like imagining I'm with a movie star. Mr. Brian is married, anyway, and all the boys in youth group have a crush on his blond wife. And he had a special smile for me when I went off with Mrs. Fellows without complaining or even rolling my eyes like some of the other kids did.

I can hear the drag of slippers shuffling towards the door, even though it's one o'clock in the afternoon. Mrs. Fellows tugs on her shirt so it doesn't bunch up around her middle. After the first house, where Mrs. Fellows did the talking, she turned to me and told me that it was my turn. Everyone wants to listen to a sweet young thing like me. So now I do the talking, though I dread the sound of the lock clicking.

I slap a smile on my face as the door creaks open. I can barely see the woman through the screen and in the dim. A smell of cigarette smoke and licorice wafts out.

"Hi, I'm from New Canaan Community Church and we'd like to give you a light bulb." I hold out a compact fluorescent on the flat of my hand, the way you offer food to a dog you don't know.

"What I got to do to get it?" Her voice is low and grating.

My smile feels stiff as Halloween wax lips. My palm is damp, like I'm going to soak through the bulb's cardboard sleeve and make a spot on the powdery glass. "Not a thing, Ma'am. It's our gift to you."

Everyone is suspicious at first. They can't believe we're giving them something for nothing. This kindness ministry is a new idea of Pastor Rob's. Pay it forward. Do a good deed and it will be returned to you a thousandfold. When I told my mother what I was doing today, she said, "That pastor is an idiot who doesn't understand the way the world works." My parents are unchurched. But I think it's a wonderful idea. A little thing like paying the toll of the person behind you on the bridge can make everybody's day brighter. It's like when I see Mr. Brian. A warm breeze passes over my heart. Giving these light bulbs away is like I'm giving these people a bit of what Mr. Brian feels like.

I like the idea, but I hate doing it. I hate the way the woman stands behind her door, looking at me like I've got a hidden knife, and I'm just waiting for her to open the screen before I spring.

"You got any regular bulbs?" she says.

I try to give away the fluorescents first, but if people don't care about killing the planet, we have the regular bulbs too. Mrs. Fellows carries those in the plastic bag strangling her wrist.

She fishes in, pulls one out by the cardboard sleeve. The sleeve has the bright yellow Let Your Light So Shine card with our church info taped to it. "Take it with God's blessing," she says, holding the light bulb toward the screen door.

"God's blessing," the woman repeats, shuffling forward. She's dressed in a pink sweatshirt with the elastic gone limp at the sleeves. Her thin, no-color hair is cut short, so it sticks up like she's buzzing with static electricity. I expect a spark when she clicks the metal screen door latch and opens the door with the toe of her slipper.

"God's blessing," she repeats, taking the light bulb in one hangnailed hand. "Where was God when my little Callie was taken from me?" The woman bangs the screen door with her hip, clanging it wide so that one pale blue slipper rests on the door frame, and one snakes out toward the dusty mat.

I jump back, but Mrs. Fellow stands her ground. "His ways are mysterious, I know," she starts, but the woman cuts in.

"Take your blessing and shove it up your ass," she says. Her voice is louder, but she's not yelling. It's worse than yelling, that scratchy voice hissing out the word "ass."

I cut a glance at Mrs. Fellows. Her face is red, but she's planted in her Velcro tennies like she's never moving. "God . . . "

"Take your God too. I haven't been in a church since Callie died, and I'm never going back, so take your goddamn light bulb and shove it up your ass too." She jerks the bulb from its cardboard sleeve and holds it towards Mrs. Fellows like a weapon. Her fingers are white along the grooved base, and her hair crackles.

"I lost my Kenny too," Mrs. Fellows says, more quietly.

"I don't give a shit. Shut the hell up and get the hell off my property." She throws the bulb at Mrs. Fellows. Mrs. Fellows jerks her head sideways, but it still hits her temple with a hollow thwok and the sparkly sound of the filaments busting before it bounces down and shatters on the cement at her feet. Mrs. Fellows seems dazed, so I grab her dry, old-lady hand and drag her off the porch, down the cracked front path to the sidewalk. I look over my shoulder, but the woman isn't following us, just standing on her doorstep in her dingy blue slippers, glass shards scattered on the mat. Still, I keep going, pulling Mrs. Fellows until we're half a block away.

Her lips are pale in the center where her coral lipstick has worn off. "Mrs. Fellows?" She doesn't seem to hear. My pulling her along has made her shirt twist crooked and popped the bottom button, revealing a spongy white triangle of skin. I don't want to touch her, but I tug at the bottom of her shirt to cover her.

She slaps at my hand. "Leave me alone." She turns her head aside. I get a good look at her temple where the light bulb hit, but I can't see any marks. She doesn't say anything else, so for a while we just stand there, not looking at each other. The lawn next to us smells like mud drying in warm sun, and above us is one of those pink-blossomed trees that smell like lip gloss. The street is empty, but a lawnmower roars somewhere, and kids yell. I close my eyes and think of Mr. Brian, his Converse high-tops, his faded jeans, the dark green polo shirt that shows his tan forearms. He'd forgotten his watch today, and I imagine licking the pale inside of his wrist. I open my eyes, my whole body hot, a tingling between my thighs. It feels sinful, but I can't stop the tingling.

Mrs. Fellows is still staring at the street. "Mrs. Fellows," I say. I'm afraid to touch her arm, in case she hits my hand away again.

"We need to pray for that lady, Misty," she says. "Pray for her right now. She has no idea about what God's about, the way He really works." And right there, standing on the sidewalk, the bag of light bulbs dangling from her wrist, she folds her hands over her belly, closes her eyes and starts. "Dear Lord, help that woman. Help to heal her pain . . . "

I pray before every meal, even though no one else in the family does, and my mom shakes her head, and my dad and my brothers just start eating. I don't mind praying while they watch me. I even sometimes open my eyes a slit to catch the look on my mom's face. But this is different. Sweat trickles down my back, and it feels like a trail of ants is walking between my shoulder blades, down to my waist and even into my butt crack. I keep listening for the drag of pale blue slippers. I fold my hands, but I keep my eyes open.

"Help her to see, as you did for me with my Kenny, that all things happen for the best." Even though Mrs. Fellows' face is calm, her eyes twitch when she says the name. Was Kenny her son? I try to imagine her with kids, but it doesn't come. I've never seen her with a husband or anyone. I never wondered about her before.

"Amen," she says suddenly, and her eyes pop open. She's calmed down some, though the hair is stuck to her forehead.

"Maybe we should just go back to the church," I say.

"No," she says, tugging at her shirt and straightening her hair carefully over the temple where the light bulb hit, "we should keep going."

"I don't want to." I can't imagine knocking on one more door, smiling one more time.

"Nonsense," she says, though her eyes still look a little twitchy.

"I'm scared," I say. I don't know whether it's true or if I'm just tired of tramping door to door and trying to give away free light bulbs.

"No one said spreading the word of God was easy."

But we aren't spreading the word of God. We're performing

an act of kindness. Kindness was supposed to be easy.

"I'm going back to the church," I say.

"Nuh-uh, Miss Misty. Pastor Rob said to give out light bulbs, and we're giving out light bulbs."

"Who's Kenny? Was he your son?"

She squints at me before saying, "He was. For a while."

For a while? What the heck does that mean? "Did he die?" But that sounds stupid. Of course he died. "Was it a car accident?"

"I'll tell you while we walk to the next place." She brushes at her thighs and turns towards the brick path that leads to the next front door.

She's half in profile, but beneath the green eye shadow her eyes are tiny and bright. Her gaspy breaths remind me of the woman at the house, as if like that woman Mrs. Fellows has been waiting for an excuse to tell her story. Just one excuse to let it all pour out. My hands start shaking and I have trouble wedging air into my lungs.

"I'm going back to the church," I say, turning my back. I walk a quick few steps, then break into a run, like I used to when I was a little kid, my hair flying behind me and the bag of light bulbs bumping against my side. It feels good to stretch my legs, to watch the sidewalk flow beneath me, the squares of concrete blur with speed. When I get near the church, I stop running to let my breath slow. My forehead is wet and I wonder how bad my armpits smell. I step into a little concrete pathway between hedges where I'm shielded from the street unless someone is right across from me and looks in. I grab the hem of my shirt, flapping it back and forth to try to dry my underarms. I run my fingers through my damp hair.

It's cool between the hedges. When I was little, I had a secret place in our side yard at the base of a tall rhododendron. I could squeeze between the trunk and the fence and sit in the shady mulch of dead blossoms. I felt like I was hidden there, though no one ever came looking for me. In our house crowded with my brothers' gym shoes and tennis rackets and noise and stink, it was my own little place. In spring the deep pink blossoms seemed like something out a fairy tale, Sleeping Beauty maybe, when the cherished princess wakes to a world gone wild and colorful.

But I'm too old now to hide in the bushes. Once I stop feeling sweaty I walk back into the sunshine and take it slow for the last half block to the church. The church looks like a white two-story apartment building with a steeple tacked on the top and one round stained glass window of a dove over the altar. They've tried to make it nice inside, with dried flower arrangements on the walls and the good kind of folding chairs with brown cushions on the seats, but it's not like those fancy churches people go to in movies with stained glass saints and carved marble. It's more real.

I'm not sure anyone will be around. We were supposed to give out light bulbs for another hour. But I'm going to wait here for a ride home, instead of calling my mom. If I ask my mom to pick me up early, she'll be full of a huge load of I Told You So. Plus she's probably off at one of my brothers' soccer games. I walk through the little concrete coffee hour patio and try the side door to the sanctuary. It opens, thank goodness, so I'll have someplace to wait.

I love being in the sanctuary when no one else is. It's both holy and magical — like a Christmas tree early Christmas morning. The tinsel glitters in the darkness, and the stockings on the fireplace bulge with goodies, and the boxes mound beneath the tree. All hushed and waiting, with something special just for you. That's what the sanctuary is like, a special place, holding its breath, waiting for worshippers.

I sit in the last row of folding chairs and enjoy the silence, the sun sifting through the dust, gold alive in the air.

If only that woman would come here, she would feel the peace. She would understand that she matters. That awful scene, the broken light bulb, Mrs. Fellows' dead son, all of that seems so distant now. I'm filled with something outside myself, like I'm the light shot through with gold.

71

The door opens behind me, and Mr. Brian walks in, his hands full of light bulbs. "Misty, what are you doing here? Where's Mrs. Fellows?" I love his voice, the way it cracks a little when it goes high. Some of the boys in class make fun of Mr. Brian's voice, but I think it makes him seem more human.

"She had to go." I want to rush to him and tell him everything, about that hateful woman telling us to shove the light bulbs up our asses, about Mrs. Fellows and her dead son. He'd take me in his arms and it would be so warm, so safe. But I know he would keep giving out light bulbs for eternity, no matter what happened. So I keep my mouth shut.

"So did Sean," he says, speaking of the guy from youth group who was paired with him. "Baseball practice." He waves a couple of light bulbs. "I thought I'd put some of these to use. Maybe you can hold the ladder for me."

The light fixtures above the folding chairs are gold metal with a yellow center, like glass-bottomed offering plates. We drag away the folding chairs, their feet sighing across the carpet. Then he unfolds the stepladder, its aluminum gleaming silver in the sunshine. He climbs up, light bulb in one hand, while I anchor the other side of the ladder, pushing hard with both hands so that it doesn't sway as he climbs. I watch his polo shirt go past, then his faded jeans. I don't look at his crotch, but even as I turn my eyes aside I see his long, hard thighs, then the denim worn pale at his knees, then his tennis shoes, not the stupid Velcro ones that Mrs. Fellows had, but really cool black All Stars. I don't think I've ever been happier in my life than I am right now, holding the ladder for Mr. Brian.

Any moment, I think. Any moment he'll look down and see me, and our eyes will meet. I feel hot all over, like earlier, hot and tingling and like I could cry or shout. It's a river of glory running through me, the same rush as when the organ plays "Ride On, King Jesus" and we all start to sing.

And then he does look down, burned bulb stretched out to

hand to me. Our eyes meet, and everything inside me rushes forth. "I love you." The words come out strong and sure. My heart is beating so hard it's shaking my hands.

"Will you take this?" he says, eyes skittering back to the lamp. I take the light bulb. It's warm from his hand.

"I love you," I say again, but this time it's all trembly. I clamp onto the metal until it digs into my palms.

He screws in the new bulb and keeps pretending to twist it even after it's as tight as it can go. I know he heard me. I'm just a kid holding the ladder for him.

Finally he clanks down the steps while I stare at the ladder feet digging into the dusty blue carpet. The ladder shifts and lightens, suddenly empty and lifeless. My face is burning, so I keep it turned away.

I turn my back, busy myself with the folding chairs. His hand touches my shoulder. "I can take it from here," he says.

I nod, not turning, and head for the door, banging into folding chairs, tipping one over as I go.

Outside it's warm compared to the church. I start to run like a hurt bird zigzagging across the ground. I find my way out of the courtyard, the air against my face cooling the tears on my hot cheeks. I run for the place between bushes and hunker down in the long blue shadows, wiping my face with the back of my hand. I try to keep it quiet, but the sobs keep exploding out of me, shaking my body. The cement of the path between the bushes is cold and gritty and I rub my palms along it, loving the sting and scrape.

Finally the heaving sobs stop. I pull the neckline of my t-shirt up and wipe my eyes. I must look terrible. I don't want any of the kids from youth group, or worse yet, Mr. Brian, seeing me like this.

I hear footsteps along the sidewalk, tired footsteps that remind me of the shuffling slippers earlier. I peer under the bushes at a familiar pair of Velcro tennis shoes coming my way. I shrink into the base of the pyracantha near me, ignoring the prickly branches in my hair, willing the shoes to keep going, for Mrs. Fellows to keep her eyes straight ahead, but it's the opposite of in the church. There I felt emotion pouring out of me, reaching to Mr. Brian. Here, it's like somehow I'm pulling Mrs. Fellows' eyes towards me. She stops.

"Misty! What are you doing here?"

"Cooling off," I mumble. My mom hates it when I mumble, but Mrs. Fellows doesn't mention it. I can feel her looking at me. I don't look up.

"Come on, I'll give you a ride home," she says.

Here's the thing. I can't catch a ride from anyone else at the church without them seeing me, which would be too embarrassing. I can't call my mom without a major production on her part. Though Mrs. Fellows is the last person I want to see, she's better than any of the other choices. Still looking at the concrete, I follow her.

A plastic bag of light bulbs swings at her side, but she makes no move towards the church buildings, instead leading me straight to the parking lot.

She has one of those typical old-lady cars—some big silver boat that smells like hairspray inside. She rolls down the windows and as we leave the parking lot I hang my head out like a dog to let the wind cool my face. We're not going very fast, though, not fast enough for the wind to block Mrs. Fellows' voice.

"I'm sorry if what happened with that woman upset you," she says.

Thank you, God, thank you, God. She has no idea what really happened.

"I guess my talking about Kenny didn't help. It's just that . . . you keep quiet about something long enough, it just bursts out of you at the wrong time." The car sways past lawns and hedges. Nobody is on the streets. "I'd like to tell you about Kenny. Can I tell you about him?"

I nod without looking at her.

"He was the most beautiful boy. Just about your age. The

girls would parade past the house, hoping to catch a glimpse of him. But he was never mean about it. Would say 'Hi' real polite to all of them. He would have been all right if it wasn't for those friends of his. You know the kind. Wild."

I nod again. I do know the kind. They shoulder between kids in the school hallway, swing their lockers shut so fast the clang echoes, laugh to be heard everywhere.

"I tried to tell him how bad they were, but he looked up to them, somehow. Grounding did no good. He'd sneak out anyway. I tried everything I could, and I still couldn't stop him." I'm sure we're circling past the same pink houses and mown lawns we've passed before. She scoops wide around turns, not braking, creeping through the straight parts. It's as if the whole world around us has fallen asleep, and we're the only car on the road, circling randomly.

I imagine a kid my age with long lashes and dark hair that looks red in the sunlight. Getting into the dark car, his friend with the learner's permit behind the wheel. The way she tells it, it's like a movie, where you want to scream "Don't go in there!"

"He had a favorite gray hooded sweatshirt he wore everywhere. He was wearing it that night. I bought another one just like it for him to wear when they buried him." Her voice is calm, but I feel the hot sting of tears against my eyes again. Not the awful explosive sobs of earlier, but the tears that come from somewhere deeper, like when you're quiet, listening to music or reading a sad book.

"Did I tell you he had a pet rabbit?" Mrs. Fellows says.

The wind pulls at my hair. The car spins on through the bright, empty streets and I perform my first real act of kindness of the day. "Huh-uh," I say. "Tell me."

THE DROUGHT CYCLE

California cycles, drought and rain
and so it seemed, till I was ten, the sky
was an even Sherwin-Williams blue
left under the sun to peel and fade.
But in my driving years, always, the rain
slid down from low and tessellated skies.
It turned the roads into a hiss of tires
and standing water rayed with melted light.
Memory drowns for certain certain things,
but tangles snags of detail on its banks:
gone it seems, our curtained weekend
coituses in damp suburban rooms.
I remember only roads and only dashboards,
no eagerness for getting there too soon.

EL NIÑO

It rains three days, my father out of town,
trees across the power lines and flooded
streets. Storm drain rivers. A small boy drowned.
The power outage slows time down. Shattered
leaves. Canada geese wade the sunken lawns.
Around the mattress in my last suburban room
candlelight oranges dull realities
into damp-sheeted romance of a ship.
Time, now storm and stillness, drifts between
two ports. Tangled blankets, cheese sandwiches,
board games. We drop acid, count pomegranate
seeds. Day three the roof begins to leak. Time is
metal drip-sound in a pan. Cool-fingered hands.
The lights come on, and we're in sight of land.

POOR VISIBILITY

10:00 pm, we come weary with our sack
of tired questions slung
over our parent backs, peddling pain
into the fall night chill;
these quarter moon queries,
yellowing no avail . . .
which we keep at,
approaching the first anniversary
empty-handed on the dam.

When and where did you enter?
How did you navigate the swamp?
Through woods, without light?
How cold the water must have been —
the downpour streaming your cheeks,
how could you see?
Whatever was the hour?
Did no
other path lead away from the water?

Listen: the language of witness trees,
wind over glassy waves, slap-syllabled shore,
cloud-troubling asides, hardening stare of stars,
hands wrought in wrung branches,
gossiping weeds cracking up the dam's concrete.
Then finally, a rising hysteria of rain
in fists and gusts,

giving me a tongue-lashing
for asking anything.

SATURN DISCUSSES HOW TO DEVOUR YOUR CHILDREN

after Rubens

There is no easy way to do this. Find
the darkest cave, the one still cluttered
with elk bones, bludgeoned skulls gaping
in the torchlight. Start with the angriest son,
his meat marbled and tenderized by fighting.
Start with his right arm, the good arm,
arm that's bundled sheaves of wheat
like the limp necks of pheasants. His hands
will be the hardest to take down. Begin
with the index finger, forefinger, the final crunch
of thumb. Dip the pinky in honey. Lap
your tongue around the wrist bone
as if rimming the last barrel
of wine. Lose yourself until your eyes bulge
like the bellies of bulls (drink madly while you do this).
Next, salt the torso three times and let
it sit while your strong tooth slices the head.
Fork the penis. Remember: *this must be done.*
Remember that dream about an overthrow,
the way he pointed that spear like Uranus' wagging tongue?
Let him kick all the way down your intestine.
Relax. We're six thousand years away
from therapists. Close your eyes.
Think of your mother placing the sickle

in your hand. Think of Rhea washing her legs.
You were young once, too. *Relax.*
You don't have to apologize.

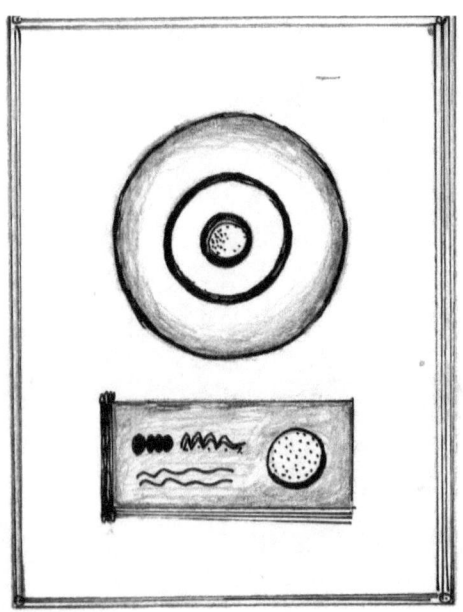

And one night in 1990, they escorted me outside the Pub
and presented me with a copy of their first gold album.

SEEKING SOLACE

— for Lisa, Colby, and Lydia

One week after the 2016 presidential election, I stopped the show at an Indigo Girls concert in Santa Fe when I called out between songs, "Thank you from Marisa at Little Five Points Pub." From the stage, Amy Ray and Emily Saliers gazed mystified in my direction, where I sat with my best friend in the tenth row.

"Marisa?" Amy said. "What are you doing here?"

"Listening to you," I said. I waved my hand high, in the event that they could discern it in the dark beyond the stage lights.

Our conversation went on for rather a long time, considering they had the rest of the show to do. I introduced them to Lisa, and when I told them I taught at UNM, Lisa clarified that we lived in Albuquerque, which garnered some applause.

"We really do know her, y'all," Emily assured the crowd.

"I found something you wrote for us not long ago," Amy said, "some dialogue. Do you remember?"

I'd written a lot of things for them in those early years, but from what Amy described, I knew exactly what she was talking about. I used to bring my journal to their shows and scribble down the funniest of their exchanges between songs. Eventually I compiled them to share as a gift.

"I photocopied it and gave it to some friends," she said.

Guitars strapped over their shoulders, both Amy and Emily continued to stare in the general direction of my seat. I knew they couldn't see me, but what I detected in their expressions was the time travel we three had embarked on. Together we were reliving

1987, 1988, 1989, and the first few years after they became famous. Amy began to talk about those times in Atlanta, those three-set performances that lasted well into the wee morning hours night after night, week after week, month after month, when they were the bar band at the Little Five Points Community Pub and drawing bigger and bigger crowds.

Now I welcomed them to New Mexico. I thanked them for their music. I asked them please to carry us through the next thirty or forty years, fifty if they could swing it.

Eventually, they played their next song.

Three days later, on the tenth day after the election, I called my mother. Our last few conversations had been tense, treacherous. She'd been "worried" about me, as she'd claimed in numerous text messages, and I might have appreciated the sentiment if her worries had any relationship to my own. In fact, her worries were a way of voicing her disapproval of my reaction to the election's outcome. I'd been in a state of anxiety nearing a full-blown panic attack, and I was trying to heal myself by working out a course of action and a course of activism. In our two previous conversations, my mother, an avid supporter of the new president-elect, had tried to soothe my worries by calling him a "blowhard" and reassuring me that his pussy-grabbing boasts were no more than "locker room talk." A retiree of nearly two decades, she'd added that she'd voted for him because of "jobs. We need jobs." I'd told her I knew he was a blowhard, but by running his campaign on a rhetoric of hatred and bigotry, he'd emboldened others to threats and acts of violence. My mother, who'd felt the need to say many times over the course of the election season that she was "not a bigot," wouldn't hear me out when I reminded her of his hate-fueled denunciations of Mexicans and Muslims, African-Americans, disabled people, women. "Just give him a chance," she said. Yes, she had repeated every cliché of his campaign and supporters. She added, "I gave

Obama a chance. I had no choice." I decided to bring up the vice-president-elect's discriminatory policies against the LGBTQ community. My mother hadn't heard about them. "I've never researched a politician in my life," she said, and, inexplicably, "I didn't know it was such a derogatory thing to be gay."

So when I called her that Friday, I was glad to have the Indigo Girls concert to talk about. She detected the lightness in my tone right away and said how good it was to hear me doing better. And she started asking about the early days of our friendship; they were the kinds of questions you would ask about something you were learning about for the first time.

"Those were some hard years," my mother said.

"Those were great years," I said.

A matter of perspective, I suppose. In May 1987, I had moved to Atlanta, and in November my parents came to visit for the Thanksgiving holiday. I invited them to join me that Wednesday night to go hear an excellent band, the two members of whom were becoming my friends. When I told them my new girlfriend would meet us there as well, my mother exploded, called me all sorts of names, and disowned me on the spot. She and my father had arrived only a few hours before, and now they were leaving. I'd come out to them earlier that year, and that had gone miraculously well, with only a modicum of drama, but what now tipped my mother into rage was that I had the nerve not only to be gay but to act on it—sexually, that is. Not only did the visit end with my mother insisting that I was no longer welcome in their home, but, she added, I was no longer welcome in our home state of Mississippi either. That night I went out alone, and when I spoke with Emily after the show and she wished me a happy Thanksgiving, she picked up on my distress and inquired. I pulled up my butchest bravest self and recounted the highlights of the argument with my parents. It must have been close to two o'clock in the morning. Emily invited me to join her and her parents and her three sisters for dinner the next day.

I would spend the next three holiday seasons with the Saliers family.

Back at the bar, the Indigo Girls put me on their permanent guest list. They liked having me in the audience because I was loud and joyful in my enthusiasm and my cheers roused others to join in. They invited me to travel with them; I joined them in Chapel Hill, New Orleans, Athens, and other places in Georgia. I sang with them on a handful of occasions and once smoked onstage to lend atmosphere to their rendition of "Summertime." I made my best friends in their crowd—and some of my best girlfriends too. And though I sometimes met Emily or Amy for coffee or lunch and conversation, we lived out most of our friendship between sets and after hours in the bars they played at in Atlanta. We exchanged gifts. I compiled the photos I took of them in albums, one for each of them. I gave Amy a pair of old Catholic medals that had belonged to my grandmother and Emily a thin gold bracelet that she wore for years without taking off. And one night in 1990, they escorted me outside the Pub and presented me with a copy of their first gold album, a way of saying thanks for always being there, always believing.

The morning after the election, my mother texted me: "I'm worried about you. How are you doing?"

I thanked her for asking and wrote, "I'm getting ready for work. My freshmen are turning in research papers today. I'm going to do what has to be done and then offer to speak with those who need to know who their allies are . . . I will show love and strength to those who have always had my back."

"Remember me," my mother replied; "I've always had your back—always will!" She added two pink hearts for emphasis.

I stared at her lie and fumed with resentment and did not respond.

The last time I saw the Indigo Girls before they left for California to make their first record for Epic was after one of their shows. We were backstage at the Fox Theatre, and I'd been talking to Emily's parents while she and Amy visited with other friends and musicians. When Emily finally wandered over, I grabbed her hands and said, "I need to tell you something before you make your record." I asked if they'd be recording her newest song, an upbeat crowd-pleaser called "Closer to Fine." Yes, they would, and in fact, it would become their first hit song and one they played at every show thereafter. I kept hold of her hands to impress upon her the urgency of what I had to say. "Then you need to learn how to pronounce solace correctly. It's solace," I said, "not soulless. Soulless means something else. Now say it with me: Solace, solace."

"Solace," she said, grinning. And that was how she pronounced it on the record, and that's how she has pronounced it ever since.

Over the years, I've often thought how fitting a word that one is, solace, for what she and Amy offered so many of us. Their performances were the backdrop to our lives, their music our soundtrack. The nights they played, the bars they played in transformed into sanctuaries, places where being queer was not only safe but it was also celebrated. Magical, an ex-girlfriend recently called those nights in the late 1980s at the Little Five Points Community Pub, and she was right, they were magical. They were also formative. I could be anyone and anything I wanted on those nights, without the risk of censure or rejection. I could be exactly myself.

FROM A FEW BAD SEEDS

Persephone knew her marriage would be hell
from the beginning, knew the man she had
and that his not so subtle flaws were there
until death do them part. She was lucky.
My Nana knew nothing about the man
her parents chose for her until her veil
was lifted. But even after the decades
she spent with him, filled with his shouting,
his drinking, women, and apologies,
she clung to that thin golden branch of vows,
a marriage that had become an overripe
pomegranate filled with a thousand seeds
of crimson hate, and cried the day he died.

KAY COSGROVE AND LAUREN HILGER

LONG LIFE TO US BOTH

I let the baby bite a raw steak.
I expect this from myself—I expect
to act in tolerance, in animal printed slacks.
My reflection caught like prey in the glass.

My eyes tonight in the waiter's tray. I'm far away
from the answer, yet I reply, Happy New Year
from the top of me. That old lie, what was it?
It's gone, though I haven't released the line.

Outwardly the truth, but just a party.
Surface phenomena. Less than money.
I snap time until the whole band gets it
perfect. The goal of doing that work comes out

as me versus everyone in eye sight.
I could have just bowed with awe,
could have been taken as a gift.
I mean to leave alone tonight. To start the year

not as the correcting me,
but as kitten to the band.
In my swan song I am the swan
with a new vocabulary. Rich with order. Thorough.

SCRAPS (LAETITIA)

I've had a habit of jotting
    half thoughts and quarter thoughts
and dream shreds since my youngest
    memories of pencil and pad
and I have some left in a stale wicker

    drawer that has long lost
the dresser it lived in. They unfold in
    my fingers like moths and eat
the fabric of the past, of the night and flit
    toward any source of light to thrum
their fragile bodies to powder against
    it. They are not dated. Uneven tongues
pulled from my own fortune-cookied mind. What
    did I mean when I wrote, *This cold rips*
the songs on my radio? I can guess now, but I can't

    guess then. My child hand wrote macabre
little lines like: *I'm a little kitty kitty put me in*
    a box and *I dreamt of a tree with torn clothes*
pinned to it and a sign that said "Peter Pan's Corner"
    and I knew it was where children were eaten
by a tiger. How did I know? Oh little me, why leave
    such artifacts of someone so long dead
that used to be me? Why make me ask if something
    can be a found poem if I wrote it in the first
place? My fingers are too large, my nails too dull

to unfold each note. Who was I writing to?
Was it this me all along, some telescoped self
out beyond the tall buildings and the fog
off the sound? Spread across the floor, I can hear
the higher pitch of my younger voice
trying to whisper, but not hush enough to keep
older me from overhearing from thirty
years due west: *The sunset feels blank.* I know. I
know exactly how you mean, but I'm not sure
I did even a year ago.

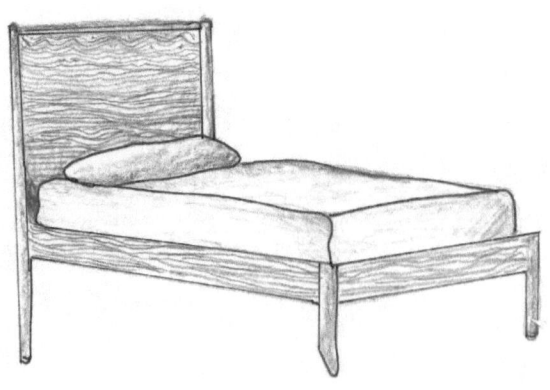

Well, under the circumstances, I mean who are we
as modern Westerners to feel like we should have
our own bed as a kind of ideal.

THE SEARCH FOR HOUSING

Act One

Group House, Mount Pleasant. $500 a month. Two women (JOANNE, SALLY), one man (GENE), and one off-screen man (TREV). JOANNE is a tech nerd, probably does data compiling for a nonprofit; SALLY is single, progressive; for a living she does social work or community organizing; GENE is a lawyer, has slight crush on SALLY; SALLY would describe GENE as "like a brother"; TREV is every bro you've ever met.

Gene: And so I'm really going to miss Allen. He was a great roommate, even if he always was hoarding all the cups in his room. That's how my month went, just a bit of anxiety about how the new person might change house dynamics.

Joanne: Thank you, Gene. I think we're all hoping our next roommate is a good fit, and doesn't stack dirty dishes, right? So, that concludes the emotional check-ins portion of our house meeting. Anything new to add to the agenda. I've got on the dry erase board: chore wheel, that's Gene, and housemate search update, that's everyone but I'm leading.

Gene: Chore wheel is . . . I just wanted to make sure I still did taking out the garbage rather than be on the chore wheel, even when the new guy comes. I hate cleaning bathrooms.

Sally: We noticed.

Joanne: Okay then, noted, (*typing and speaking stilted*) Gene. wants.

to. stay. off. chore. wheel. When-the-new-guy-comes. (*looks up*) So, the new housemate. I've set up an email account, posted the ad to craigslist and got people to fill out a little survey to make it easier and, well, so far we've gotten over 800 responses.

Gene whistles.

Sally: Oh man.

Joanne: But don't worry, I've made all the data searchable so that we can sort through them for the traits we want, so we don't have to read them all.

Sally: Well, it should definitely be a guy, you know, keep a gender balance.

Joanne: Okay, easy, down to only 300 already.

Sally: About our age, give or take a few years.

Joanne: Like, how close?

Sally: I don't want to be with anyone going through their 20s, or if you're over 40 and still want to be in a group house. I don't know, isn't that odd? Maybe if they're really early in their 40s it's not *that* weird. But we can be picky. Say 38 max?

Joanne: Okay, 30 to 38.

Sally: 31.

Joanne: (*looks mildly suspicious, then gives Indian head bob*): Fine, 31 to 38. To narrow it more, and we probably don't want anyone without a stable job or kids or pets.

Sally: I agree totally. Even really a relationship if we can avoid it. You know if it's someone who is going to have someone over so much and staying over, now we've got a 5 person group house.

Joanne: Yeah. Even if they spend all their time at the other's place, then we don't get to know them, and they are not going to be invested in the chore wheel or house dinner, or house movie night.

Sally: We want someone who's going to be open to watching *The Notebook* during a snowstorm, and not complain with all this masculine bullshit about how it's a chick-flick, and so can't see it for the classic it so clearly is. (*looks at Gene*)

Gene: It's not even a good movie. Objectively.

Sally: You say 'objectively' when you mean 'subjectively.' It doesn't improve your argument as much as you think. Anyway, how would you know? You didn't stay through it.

Gene: He dangled himself from a ferris wheel until she agreed to a date with him, while she was on a date with another guy. That's not romantic, that's objectively . . . emotional terrorism.

Sally: Ryan Gosling can do what he wants.

Gene: That's . . . (*can't find words*)

Sally: What, you don't think Rambo or whoever isn't committing actual terrorism when he goes into third world countries guns-a-blazing? (*shoots fingers*) Pew-pew.

Gene: That's your argument? Finger guns?

Sally: My argument is that it's a guilty pleasure. Don't analyze my lizard brain unless you want me to analyze yours. (*shoulder shrugs*)

Joanne: Okay, stop, guys. I can't sort by movie tastes anyway. You'll need to ask that at the interview stage. Is that all?

Sally: He needs to be tall.

Others look at her, now openly suspicious.

Sally: What? We need someone who can reach those top shelves. Or that spider above the sink. Who even knows what's up there. There could be gold or messages from tall former housemates, back when we had those.

The others continue to look at her.

Sally: Guys, I'm not going to try to date him. It would be like incest to date a housemate, but cute guys have cute male friends. They travel in packs, and they all look alike. Aaand, I can date his friends. New roommate is going to help me find Man Sally.

Gene's eyes sadden a little at "incest," but blanks it out with a head shake when he realizes he's doing it.

Joanne: Man Sally?

Gene: Not "Man Sally" again.

Joanne (*looks at Gene*): You know about this?

Gene: Too much.

Joanne: Why don't I know? Who's Man Sally? You guys have in-jokes I'm not in on now? That's not allowed.

Sally: It's not an "in-joke." Man Sally is how I describe my ideal partner. He's like me, but the man version. And this new roommate is going to help me find him. Our new roommate is going to be Man Sally's friend and make the connection.

Gene: He doesn't need to be tall. We have a stool. In the kitchen. By the shelves.

Sally: But who can find it? (*leans back and waves her hand*) It's never where it's supposed to be because you keep moving—

Gene: I don't keep moving it and, anyway, I just want to note, for the record, that while I support getting a guy for gender balance, that we are supposed to be liberals. And the criteria Sally just described literally just recreated every form of housing discrimination that we've fought against for the past 50 years or so. Aren't we being a tad hypocritical in our criteria? We're just going to end up with someone who's exactly like us.

All have a silent, awkward moment, sorta noting their own skin and features.

Sally: Lettttt'sss not get too reflective about this, okay, unless you think craigslist will take down our ad and come after us?

Gene (*sighs*): No. They'd have to take down almost every ad.

Joanne: So, I've put in what I'm going to call "Sally's OK Cupid profile search parameters."

Sally: Look, I don't even care if he's gay. I'm just saying who I want to live with.

Joanne: As I was saying, I've put in "Sally's dating profile search parameters" and we still have . . . eighty options.

Sally mouths "Oh my God," gives silent clap.

Joanne: Why is our rent so low and attractive to strangers? Can't we have one fewer roommate and all pay a little more?

Gene: Fine, we violate the Fair Housing Act. Whatever. Anyway, there's probably an exception if you're going to live with the person.

Sally: Let's add "no more lawyers, unless they are always going to take my side when Gene starts mentioning statute six seven eight blah blah." (*mimics talking with hand*)

Gene: I never cite statutes.

Sally: Yes, but I can hear you thinking them to yourself.

Joanne: So, do you want to hear my criteria, which I don't think violate housing laws? I've also come up with my list of traits I want our ideal roommate to have.

Sally: Okay cool.

Joanne: First, I want them to be able to jump a curb with a bike.

Sally: Wait, what? Can you sort for that?

Joanne: I may have included the question in the survey. Anyway, we all ride bikes here, right? We've got a whole hallway full of bikes. Nothing but bikes as far as the eye can see.

Sally: How do we test that? Is that part of the interview? Can they bring their own bike?

Joanne: It'll be fun. It'll make the interview less awkward. This is important: 25% of the energy in the house is going to change. And this is our chance to collectively steer the house towards a particular culture, so we need to be honest about what's important to us in a roommate. I want bikers who aren't just all "I bike fast," I want people who are interested in doing cool things with their bikes.

Sally: Hopping a curb is not really that hard. Maybe we should have them do it on the tandem, alone.

Joanne (*eyes go wide*): Yes. Or the first round they are alone on the tandem, then we keep adding people. Or they have to jump the curb on the tandem bike with each housemate to test compatibility, coordination.

Gene: Now that is definitely a housing rights —

Joanne: No no. No violation. You just hate how much space the tandem takes up in the hallway. Anyway, I made an "explain why you can't" option if they can't. If they're disabled they're exempt from the Tandem Test.

Sally: I'm totally down with that one. What's next?

Joanne: Okay, two: they have to beat us one-on-one in Scrabble.

Gene: Fine, but they get to choose who they challenge and that will tell us something too.

Sally: Actually I want him . . . hmmm . . . I want him to always

99

let me win at the game but I don't want him to let me know that he's letting me win at the game, so that I'm tricked into thinking I'm better at all games than him. That's right.

Gene: Are we talking about our new roommate or Man Sally?

Sally: Both. They should both always lose to me.

Joanne (*typing*): Okay, so he has to beat either Gene or me if he picks one of us, but lose to Sally if he picks her.

Gene: You can code for that?

Joanne: No. That's just a note for the interview, in case we reach the "obstacle course stage." Okay, my next one. I want them to like Dirty South rap. Is that too specific?

Sally: I don't know what that is.

Joanne: You know, Bounce, Trap . . . Dirty South.

Blank stares from the other two.

Joanne: Some people include Outkast, though they are sort of their own thing.

Sally: Maybe a bit more open, or we can use it as a tie-breaker? Like what if they are from DC, and they like Go-go music?

Joanne: What's Go-go music? No, it has to be Dirty South.

Sally (*rubs hands together, moves herself next to or behind Joanne so that they both see the screen*): Okay, what are we down to?

Joanne (*clicks laptop*): Two responses.

Sally: Excellent, maybe we can interview them both.

Joanne: Okay. Here's the first one's cover letter:

New male actor TREV reads in background:

Trev: "Hey future homies! My name's Trev. I saw your ad on craigslist! I'm clean, tall, financially stable."

The two women exchange positive nods.

Trev: "Dad's in finance but I wanted to do politics, love to work out, cycling, and swimming. I just did my 5th Iron Man—woot!"

Gene: He's such a bro. Everything about him.

Sally (*a little uncertain*): He bikes.

Gene (*smug*): I bike. Trev "cycles." Probably wearing spandex and clip-ins, always traveling in a pack shouting at people in the park. (*grunts, raising volume*) On your right!

Sally: Whatever. Anyway, keep going.

(Gene looks a little stung.)

Trev: "I can even offer to pay a couple months rent up front if it seems like a good fit (despite all the estrogen—lol). I'm looking for a place in the area because I'd like somewhere close to the Capitol where I can be around other young people. I don't know many people on the east coast other than a few of my old USC Sig Ep brothers who now work 'on the street' (money, not drugs, lol)."

Women's faces grow increasingly uncomfortable. Sally winces a bit at the word "estrogen," eventually spoiling into a gagging face.

Trev: "I'm looking to make some friends that also like the outdoors and maybe even shredding some weak sauce waves at Virginia Beach—haha, jk—but I could teach you guys to surf. Oh, my job: I just moved from Cali to work on the Trump 2016 campaign."

Sally (*clutches arms of chair or back of Joanne's chair*): Stop. Nope. Nope. No more.

Trev (*loud at first, then fading as he leaves stage*): "MAGA! MAGA! MAGA. MAGA."

Gene (*clearly pleased*): Wait, keep reading, I want to see what he has to say about Dirty South music.

Sally: Nope. Don't care. Don't want to ruin it. Don't need to hear more.

Gene: You two can go to sick shows together. A little Trap, a little Sublime, maybe some Dave Matthews. It'll be cute. Maybe he's like the Ryan Gosling of Trump supporters.

Sally: Doesn't matter. Nope.

Joanne: Maybe door number two. Out of over 800 people seeking DC, my algorithm says this one guy is our best match.

Joanne clicks dramatically in an affected gesture as Sally peers curiously over her shoulder. Gene watches in suspense.

Both women: Ohhh.

Both woman immediately recoil. Sally turns away but can't help sorta looking through fingers.

Gene: What? What?

Joanne: Well, he seems to have filled out the survey at random, he didn't put anything in the cover letter except . . .

Sally: It's a dickpic. No cover letter, no anything, his whole application is just a dickpic.

Gene: Alright, let's bring him in. Spreadsheet says he's the perfect applicant. Let's, see how he does on the bike test.

Act Two

Room in DIVORCEE's Brownstone, Takoma Park. $450 a month. KIM – mid-20s woman, DIVORCEE – 55+ year-old woman.

The two walk on stage together.

Kim: The room looks great. I love the farmer's market.

Divorcee: It would be great to have a younger person in here. Since the divorce and the kids leaving for college, the space . . .

Kim: But there is one thing that I'll need to share with you from the outset.

Divorcee: Go ahead.

Kim: I'm in an ENM relationship.

Divorcee: What's that?

Kim: An ethical non-monogamous relationship. I have a primary partner, and a secondary partner, but everyone knows about each other and we have agreed. It's usually just the same two or three people, and I don't want you to thinking I'm cheating if you see me come in and out with —

Divorcee (*smokes cigarette*): Cheating. (*chuckles*) Honey, I've lived in Takoma for forty years, from before we banned nuclear weapons. You're just now joining a community that I've been in for years. I *know* what an *ethically non-monogamous* relationship is. A lot of people in Takoma Park seem to love ethical non-monogamy more than they hate nuclear-proliferation. What's your name again?

Divorcee enunciates the words "ethical non-monogamy" each time she says them.

Kim: Kim.

Divorcee (*smiles oddly*): You been together long, Kim? You and your primary partner?

Kim: Six months? Eight?

Divorcee (*exhales cigarette in affected manner*): Here's how I feel about ethical non-monogamy: I think it's the height of liberal smugness. Oh, don't give me that look. I marched with King and I voted for Nader, twice. I don't mind if you do it. My objection is to the term "ethical." What's so ethical about it? Why can't you just call them "open relationships?" But no, they have to be ethical, so ethical.

Kim: I'm sorry, I don't follow.

Divorcee: It's smug. You're are putting a moral qualification on a category. You're implying you've discovered some new morally superior way to get your rocks off. How does anyone know? As though no old-fashioned affair ever destroyed a miserable marriage. As though these new couples never play mind games or manipulate. Humans aren't good enough beings to bring moral requirements into whole categories of relationships. That's what I say. Me, if I ever get in a relationship again, I'm going to let them know that I prefer unethical monogamy. That way I can be as emotionally withholding as I want, and I can say the warning was right there in the title.

Kim: I didn't mean to offend. I can call it something. I was more worried you might object on religious grounds or —

Divorcee (*gives wry smile*): Honey, do I seem religious to you?

Kim: I . . . maybe? I don't know. You mentioned All Souls.

Divorcee (*laughs*): All Souls is Unitarian. That's barely church. I don't object. You know, the way you kids talk, you'd think you kids invented sex, but we were trying out stranger things in the sixties. Thinking free love was free. Kim, I'm 58 years old. I've had four husbands and five marriages, that'll be on my tombstone. My third husband, Stanley, Stanley was the best. Nice mustache, a bit old, but a good lover. He brought me flowers a week after his wife of 35 years died. Not even long enough for the cusp of respectability. (*exhales smoke*) And I knew he was going to do it, come by, took him right in. His wife had been sick, not fully there anymore, and he hadn't had a companion in a while. He'd be friendly at the farmer's market. Just showed up at my door when most people said he should have been mourning. (*sighs*) What were we talking about?

Kim: My boyfriends. So you don't mind my partners coming around?

Divorcee: Bring whoever you want around.

Kim (*relaxes*): That's so great to hear. I can't afford more than this.

Act Three

Group House, Bloomingdale. $500-$600 a month, depending. INTERVIEWER ONE, INTERVIEWER TWO, and APPLICANT can all be any mix of genders/ages.

All three laughing.

Interviewer One: I love going to Goodwill. Like that feeling when I come across someone's inside joke that they discarded.

Applicant: I know exactly what you mean. Once saw this jacket with all these random patches sewn on it, of Kim Kardashian's face with Steve Buscemi eyes. So creepy that I almost had to buy it. Oh, I remembered what I wanted ask you: Do you guys ever go to see Granny and the Boys?

Interviewer One: At Showtime? That's our favorite place. That's our jam.

Applicant: Oh, this interview is going so well, I feel comfortable saying out loud how well this interview is going. You guys are just so cool, I love how you decorated the place. (*looking around*) And you do infused gins. Even the bottles look . . . so cool.
Interviewer One: So, the issue is, there is one thing.

Interviewer Two: Yes, one thing, it's really low rent, right? For the area.

Applicant (*still happy, but wary*): Amazing rent. How do you do that? Old lease? Landlord lives in Albuquerque.?

Interviewer One: Not exactly. The way our group house works, it was more expensive, but we decided to save on costs. We have two more housemates than we have beds. So, 6 beds, 8 people.

Applicant: I . . . how does that work? Are some roommates couples?

Interviewer One: No. No. No. Nobody is dating. We rotate.

Applicant: You rotate sharing beds with people you're not dating. Isn't that uncomfortable? Like you have to spend the night trying not to cross an imaginary line down the bed?

Interviewer Two: It goes fairly smoothly, actually, and it really saves on costs. Do you know how hospital matching programs work for doctors?

Applicant: Vaguely?

Interviewer One: So it's just like that. We had this one guy, Ashten, he was good with programing and he put together a formula. Everyone picks the rooms they want the most, and the people. You do it anonymously, you get absolute veto for up to two people, and if you end up sharing you automatically get a bigger bed and lower rent. Then every two months we switch. It's like pareto optimal.

Applicant: I'm pretty sure pareto optimal bedding would involve more beds.

Interviewer One: Well, under the circumstances, I mean who are we as modern Westerners to feel like we should have our own bed as a kind of ideal. Throughout history most people were lucky with some hay to sleep on.

Interviewer Two: And sometimes it works out really well. Like Ashten was a medical student so he was barely home and the person he shared with was a night shift guy over at 9:30 Club so they barely overlapped. Or you would think you would want to be sleeping alone but then when you're not chosen for a while you start to feel left out. You start asking, do people not like me? Am I the person everyone is vetoing?

Applicant: So everyone kind of loses? Can't I just sleep on the couch? Like this couch looks comfortable?

Interviewer One: No. No. No. The couch is communal.

Applicant: Then like sharing a room but not a bed. Like two twin beds maybe?

Interviewer Two: Do you want to pay for that?

Applicant (*winces*): Not really. So, are you guys, like a sex cult? Because the ad didn't mention—

Interviewer One: No. No. No. This is just sleeping-sleeping.

Interviewer Two: Yeah, we have a different spreadsheet for that. I mean, come on, someone might snore but be a beast in the bedroom.

Matt Duggan

WHEN FOXES COME OUT TO PLAY

I rise before the dew
when the snails and crickets
race to the side-lines of the back garden;

Where stale pieces of tandoori chicken
plastic rind are resting on a party plate for the foxes —
I watch the night turn into day and my eyes turn
into giant blue turtle lights;

I watch them play in the opposite garden
The lawn is measured and cut to exact perfection;
As I see him watering his land for hours into days.

When the foxes come out to play — on his immaculate green
wrestling and biting digging up his perfectly lined pitch.

I should really do the neighbourly thing
disturb them from their playing but it's so beautiful to see
fox cubs having so much fun — rolling in the amber sun playing
   as they should.

NIAGARA FALLS VS. THE HEADWATERS OF THE MISSISSIPPI

In my personal brackets they always
make it to the finals, and I always
choose the headwaters. Pretty big upset,
I know. The Falls: epic and breathtaking,
there's just something about them makes you want
to paint an enormous, roaring canvas,
open a chain of casinos, build a wax
museum, or throw up some chemical
plants and spew a little toxic waste into
the ground water. You see those falls, you feel
the mist, you want to buy souvenirs
or climb into a barrel. It's the Lamborghini
of natural wonders, it's God's own Super
Bowl halftime show. The headwaters is
a 94 Honda Civic with AM radio,
so modest, so defiantly unspectacular, the great
white explorers and surveyors, Cass
and Brower, refused to believe the mighty
Mississippi starts in a quiet corner of
Itasca, this utterly ordinary lake, a slow
knee-deep spill that only later, miles
downstream, becomes a strong brown
god. No, Brower said. Too small.
And yet, that's where I want to be poured
out on some quiet summer morning, my boys
with their pants rolled up, tapping out my gray ashy

self, waving to me and smiling, as I begin to flow,
a 90-day trip down river to a place I've never been.

MY MOTHER'S WOODEN SPOON

I keep it in a clear tub, neatly labelled
"Childhood," my mother's wooden spoon, darkened
now with age, like a vintage baseball bat.
She spent her last months crippled by MS, ankles
swollen like balloons, her heart and kidneys
failing, confined to an adjustable
medical chair provided by the county,
positioned in our shabby dining room.
I helped my sister do what needed to be done.
There was an oxygen machine, a catheter
bag, compression socks, bottles of pills.
That spoon was always in her hand.
She used it to work the controls on her chair,
or point at what she wanted brought to her.
When she needed us, she banged it on the arm
of the chair. I could hear it, even in my bedroom,
working to write a paper, listening to music,
trying to forget who and where I was,
and I didn't always come right away.
When my sister tried to read to her
some lines from Khalil Gibran, parents
and children, archers and arrows, my mother
pointed that spoon like a weapon, silenced
what she didn't want to hear.
On the night before she died, her brother
sat at her side, flown in from Nashville
because he had a feeling. Charlie

leaned in to kiss her one last time and
she touched him on the shoulder with that spoon,
her hand a crippled claw now, something regal
about her, clutching her battered wooden scepter.
Someday my sons will have to take the lid off.
What's this? they'll wonder. Who saves a wooden
spoon? Keep or toss. They'll need to decide.

Vivian says, "Do you have enough dish towels?" and
Annie says, "We have tons," and Vivian says, "Good."

IT'S YOU

Annie moves to D.C., where in a few weeks she will start a graduate program in Literature. She is 22. She lives half a mile from campus in a row house with three roommates, strangers from the internet, one of whom is rarely around. She has never lived in a city, or a group house — she has never done a lot of things — but she likes all the weird little things about the apartment, like how the kitchen seems to have as many corkscrews as it does water glasses. Or how, in the living room, there is a five-foot tree branch suspended from the ceiling with fishing line, dotted with lights.

Four days after she moves in, one of her roommates, Frances, turns 26 and throws a dinner party to celebrate. Frances makes two lasagnas, one vegetarian and one with meat, and dumps salad mix from a giant bag into a wooden bowl. Fourteen people crowd into the living room, balancing plates on their laps, illuminated by a few dozen candles. Annie wonders how long it took to light them all. She sits on the floor, next to the non-working fireplace, sips wine from a coffee cup, and worries, vaguely, about a house fire. Conversations swirl around her, about homemade bread, a hot air balloon festival in New Mexico, the Calder exhibit at the National Gallery. "So," says a girl seated next to her. Her face is bare except for a slash of lipstick. "*You're* the new roommate."

The girl introduces herself — her name is Madeline — and explains she used to live in the house. "You're in my old room. That's why I know everything about your life."

Annie is disarmed by Madeline's directness. She is formulating a way to respond when her other roommate, Micah, stands on the

115

coffee table and taps a fork against a juice glass brimming with wine. He tells a story about the dinner party Frances hosted for her last birthday: she misfired opening a bottle of champagne and the cork hit an overhead light fixture, sending shattered glass into the food. "We ordered Chinese," Micah says. He raises his glass. "To Frances. May she avoid champagne."

Micah brings out a plate of Hostess cupcakes pricked with candles and everyone sings — Annie hums, not trusting her voice. She pours white wine into her cup, forgetting there's already red in it. Then she rises a little unsteadily and slips out of the room, up the stairs, into her bed.

There are still two weeks before classes start. The days are long. Annie paints a wall in her bedroom lilac gray and wonders if Madeline, from the party, would approve of the color. She reads a story collection about girls who transform into wild animals — a rhinoceros, a cheetah, a snake — and bakes banana bread, cutting it into slices, arranging them on a plate in the kitchen for her roommates. She tries to ignore the sensation she is waiting — waiting for classes to begin, to make friends, to determine if her decision to move to this unfamiliar place was a good one or a bad one.

To distract herself, she walks four miles to the National Gallery. She arrives at the West building drenched in sweat and takes the people mover to the East building, passing through a tunnel that looks like the night sky, star-dappled with LCD lights. She goes to the museum café, where she buys a $4 bottle of water, and then finds the Calder room. She stands beneath a mobile, looking up. It drifts slowly, almost imperceptibly.

That night, Annie goes to her father and stepmother's house in suburban Maryland for dinner. They moved there two years ago, for what her father calls a *fresh start*. Annie's mother remains in Ohio, where Annie grew up.

She takes two buses and walks for a mile to get there, to

prove a point about the goodness of public transportation: doing something that takes a long time, she believes, is virtuous. She stands on the slate walkway leading to the front door and tries to decide what her roommates would think about the house. It is a white Colonial, set on a manicured lawn. Everything about it is too big, too pristine.

Inside, her stepmother, Vivian, gives her a hug and ushers her into the kitchen, where Annie's father is uncorking a bottle of wine with a *pop*. He sets the corkscrew on the counter, kisses her on the cheek, and pours the wine into three glasses the size of cereal bowls. They carry them to the dining room, where the meal is arranged on the table: baked salmon, roasted asparagus, bread. "Please," Vivian says. "Help yourself." She dims the lights, switches on two electric candles, and settles across from Annie's father, placing the cloth napkin in her lap. "How's city life?" she asks.

"Good," Annie says. She elaborates in generalities; she likes her roommates and her neighborhood. She describes what she knows of her graduate assistantship (it has not technically started yet), which involves coordinating the department's yearlong reading series.

"What is a *reading series*, exactly?" her father says.

Annie spears asparagus onto her plate. "A reading series," she says, "is where you invite writers to campus. And they *read*."

"He knows what a reading series is," Vivian says, lightly. She reaches for her glass of wine. "He's just being difficult."

Vivian seems to understand it is her role to keep the conversation going. She talks about the gym she and Annie's father go to twice a week, and the abundance of fluorescent yoga pants at the gym. Annie is grateful for her chatter. If she and her father were left to their own devices, they would just sit there, quietly chewing.

After dinner, Vivian brings out a plate arranged with grapes and squares of dark chocolate. "So," she says, plucking a grape from its stem. "Are you seeing anyone?"

Annie can tell by the way her father shifts in his seat that he is listening intently. She wipes her mouth and replaces the napkin in her lap. "Not at the moment."

"You've been so busy," Vivian says. "I suppose there's hardly time for men."

It is hard to remember a time when Annie has been less busy. "I suppose not," she says.

The next morning, Annie walks three miles to a coffee shop she read about on the internet. It is small and industrial-looking, the girl behind the counter with bangs that cut straight across her forehead and a vine tattoo crawling up her arm. Annie orders a coffee and sits on a stool in the window, wishing she had ordered something cold, wondering how she will occupy the rest of the day. She watches as two boys zip by the window on electric scooters, and as a big, brown and black dog stops to examine the base of a parking meter. On the other end of the leash is a dark-haired girl in sunglasses, a striped tank top tucked into black, wide-legged pants. She looks like an heiress with a wild streak, one who might steal the family boat and set sail for an island. It is Madeline, Annie realizes. The girl from the party.

Before she stops to think about it, Annie knocks on the window. Madeline looks up, tilts her head. She says something indecipherable through the glass, but it looks like, *It's you.* Annie finds herself standing, tossing the coffee, moving to the exit.

On the sidewalk, Madeline lifts her aviators to the top of her head. "You disappeared the other night," she says.

Annie leans down and scratches the dog's ears, avoiding eye contact. "You have a dog?" she asks, stupidly.

"Actually, my brother is supposedly dog-sitting Howard here," Madeline says. "He loves dogs but is also completely irresponsible, so."

Howard jumps on Annie, tail wagging, paws digging into her hipbones.

"He's a monster," Madeline says, yanking on the leash. "We were just on our way to the dog park. Want to come?"

The park is gravel-floored and bordered by a chain-link fence. Inside, there are six or seven dogs, ten or so humans, and three benches shaded by canvas tarps. Madeline sits on a bench and unleashes Howard, who runs back and forth along the chain-link, tongue flying alongside his mouth. A few yards away, a small, curly-haired dog bounds after a chewed up tennis ball, clamps it in his mouth, and trots to the shade. Annie is struck by how pleasant dog-watching is. Dogs are always happy, and they are never weirded out when you stare at them.

Madeline reaches into her canvas bag and pulls out a pack of gum. "My ex-girlfriend lives two blocks from here. It makes the dog park interesting."

Annie places her hand against the grainy plastic of the bench, absorbing this information. "How long ago did you break up?"

"It's been six months. But we lived together for another month, until I found a sublet."

"Yikes," Annie says.

Madeline offers a piece of gum to Annie. "Have you ever lived with someone you dated?"

The gum is cinnamon-flavored; Annie's mouth floods with saliva. If she wanted to answer the question honestly, she might say she has never really *dated* anyone. She has slept with three guys (encounters that, in hindsight, confirmed she has no interest in sleeping with guys), and she was either infatuated or in love with her freshman-year roommate, Eva. But Eva was straight—only interested in kissing girls if it involved an audience at a party, and Annie never went to parties. That is, more or less, the extent of her experience with girls. "No," she says.

"Smart," Madeline says. Her phone chimes. She fishes it from her bag and looks at the screen. "My brother is having a dinner party tonight, and he wants me to bring a chocolate soufflé." She taps on the screen and sighs. "He could never just ask me to bring dessert. It has to be something specific and impossible."

"Can you skip it?"

"I could, but he throws the best parties. Last time it was Moroccan-themed and he, like, bought a clay pot and made a four-hour tagine and decorated his studio with paper lanterns."

"Wow," Annie says.

Madeline digs her thumbnail into a mosquito bite on her knee, which is red and raw from scratching. Annie resists the impulse to reach over and place a finger on top of the bite. She allows herself to wonder how the next few hours might unfold: maybe, after the park, they will go on a long, meandering walk with Howard, and stop at a bar with a dog-friendly patio, and drink several beers under an umbrella. Maybe Madeline will invite her to the dinner party.

"Should we go?" Madeline asks.

Annie is about to say, *I would love to go*, when she realizes Madeline means should they leave the dog park. "Yes," Annie says. "Let's go."

They collect Howard and walk to the gate, and Annie tries to memorize what it is like to *be* somewhere with someone like Madeline—even if it is a dog park, and they ended up there by accident, and it will never occur to Madeline to think about it again. A piece of gravel slips inside her shoe, settling beneath her heel, but she ignores it. Madeline unlatches the lock. "You should give me your number," she says, and Annie tries to keep her voice steady as she recites it.

Madeline calls Annie's phone. "Now you have mine," she says.

That night, Annie reaches for her phone, opens her contacts, and finds Madeline's entry. She taps on Google and types *Am I*, just to see what auto-complete comes up with:

Am I pregnant

Am I gay

Am I stoned

Am I psychic

Am I happy

She sets the phone on the bookshelf, closes her eyes, and wonders if any part of Madeline remains here, in the room she used to occupy. Skin cells, maybe. A strand of hair, lodged deep between the floorboards.

Madeline does not text the next day, and she does not text the day after that, probably because she has a rich and fulfilling life, and people like Annie exist only as an afterthought. Three days after the dog park—a Wednesday—Annie's phone vibrates, and she resists looking at the screen for several seconds, anticipating Madeline's name flashing across it. But it is only her stepmother, Vivian, calling to ask if she is interested in a lightly used KitchenAid mixer. "I picked it up at a yard sale for twenty dollars," she says. "I know how much you love to bake."

"That's really nice," Annie says. "Thanks."

"I could swing by to drop it off, if you'll be around."

"Sure."

"You're not too busy?"

"Nope," Annie says.

Vivian arrives an hour later, hauling the mixer in an oversized canvas bag. She steps through the front door, sets the bag next to the couch, and takes in the living room: the hanging tree branch, the unlit candles in the non-working fireplace. It is difficult to tell whether she finds the room charming, or depressing, or neither. It occurs to Annie that in the three years they have known each other, they have never spent time together without Annie's father. She knows the basics of Vivian's life (raised in Columbus, works from home as a CPA, once divorced, no children), but little else.

"How about a tour?" Vivian says.

The tour is short. They climb the stairs and start with Annie's nest of a bedroom. Vivian walks to the bookshelf and taps on the spine of a novel about a small child living on a commune in the

1960s, a witness to a failed utopia. The book has sex and drug use and poverty disguised as a lifestyle choice. "This is one of my favorites," she says.

Annie tries to conceal her surprise. Her father is not much of a reader, and she had assumed the same was true of Vivian. "Really?"

"My mother lived on a collective farm for a few months when she was nineteen," Vivian says. "Which I find fascinating. She refuses to tell me anything about it, of course."

"Wow," Annie says.

"It's hard to imagine, isn't it?"

They return to the first floor, pass through the living room, and conclude the tour in the kitchen. "Tea?" Annie asks.

Vivian says she would love a cup. She settles on a stool at the kitchen island.

Annie puts the kettle on the stove and takes a box of tea from the cabinet. She hears the front door open and close and a moment later her roommate Frances appears in the kitchen, a tote bag slung over her shoulder. "Oh," she says, when she sees Vivian. "Hello."

"My stepmother, Vivian," Annie says. "She was just dropping off some kitchen supplies."

"I hope I'm not intruding," Vivian says.

"Not at all." Frances takes the water pitcher from the refrigerator and pours a glass. To Annie, she says, "Are you going to the game tomorrow?"

"What game?" Annie asks.

"The baseball game," Frances says. "Madeline didn't text you?"

Annie shakes her head.

"She was running around like a crazy person yesterday. She probably forgot." Frances shrugs. "Anyway, we have an extra ticket, and she wanted to invite you. She thinks you're intriguing."

"Intriguing?" Annie says. "How am I intriguing?"

"Well," Frances says, "I guess there are a lot of ways a person can be intriguing."

The kettle whistles and Annie pulls it from the stove, her

hands shaking a little as she pours the water. She thinks: *I am intriguing.*

"So you'll come?" Frances says.

"Sure," Annie says.

"Cool." Frances takes a banana from the bowl on the counter. "I have no idea what the actual plan is, but I'll let you know." She smiles at Vivian. "Nice to meet you."

"You too," Vivian says.

Frances leaves and Annie sets the cups on the kitchen island, collecting the sugar bowl and two spoons. "I think we're out of milk."

"That's okay," Vivian says.

Annie spoons sugar into her cup.

"Who's Madeline?" Vivian asks.

Annie stirs the tea. She taps the spoon against the rim of the cup and sets it on the counter. "Madeline," she says, "is a girl I like." Then she has said it, and it cannot be taken back.

"Oh," Vivian says.

In high school, Annie once saw a girl walk up to a guy in the cafeteria, pick up his tray, and hurl it across the room. The sound of the glass and metal and plastic crashing to the floor was incredibly, gloriously loud. Now, she understands what that girl must have felt like: exhilarated, strange, destructive. She waits for a sense of regret to wash over her. For one thing, it is entirely possible Vivian will go home and relay this information to Annie's father. But then, Annie feels no desire to be there when he finds out.

She looks up, at her stepmother, who does not appear to be appalled, or even surprised. "What's she like?" Vivian asks.

"She is someone who would go to a yard sale and buy a poster," Annie says. "And she would take it home and hang it on her wall and, like, a month later find out it was worth a thousand dollars."

Vivian nods. She seems to be waiting to see if Annie will say more, but Annie has said enough. Vivian says, "Do you have enough dish towels?" and Annie says, "We have tons," and Vivian says, "Good."

The next afternoon, Frances texts to say that a few people are meeting in front of the baseball stadium at 5:30 pm, and that she will head there straight from work. When Frances says a few people, what she actually means is eleven people, all loud and affable, some of whom Annie recognizes from the birthday party. Madeline arrives with a pixie-haired girl everyone else seems to know. "Hey," she says, to Annie. "Have you met Darby?"

"Hey there," Darby says.

"Hi," Annie says.

They scan their tickets and enter the stadium, climbing to the third tier, above the first baseline. Madeline sits next to Darby, an impossible five seats away from Annie. The day is hot and clear, the seats in direct sunlight. Annie realizes she forgot to put on sunscreen. She imagines the ultraviolet light penetrating her skin, radiating her. The guy next to her, Adam, taps her shoulder. "You want a beer?" he asks.

"Sure," Annie says. He returns a few minutes later with two aluminum bottles of Budweiser. "Can I give you some money?" she asks.

"How about you buy me a drink later," he says.

The beer is 16 ounces. Annie drinks it quickly, fast enough that everything starts to seem tolerable. The field is a bright, electric green, and the seats around the stadium are dotted with red jerseys, red t-shirts, red hats. She is vaguely aware of movement on the field, mostly batters walking from the dugout to home plate. "The pitcher is good," she says.

"He's really good," Adam says. "You like baseball?"

"No," Annie says. "I think baseball is terrible."

Adam laughs. Annie finishes the Budweiser and wonders if this is all flirting is: making ridiculous statements. She watches the concession runners sprint up and down the stairs, swiping credit cards, dispensing food. "Do you like hot dogs?"

"Obviously," Adam says.

She buys two hot dogs and two beers. The total is a staggering

$28, but they taste magnificent. Adam, it turns out, is an avid reader. They discuss the merits of a newish novel about a fucked-up family in Anchorage, Alaska, written by a forty-something man who used to work on a fishing boat. The novel is over 500 pages. There is a long, detailed scene in which the teenage son drinks a bottle of Robitussin, drives to a drugstore, and falls asleep with his arm in the cuff of a blood pressure machine. There is another scene in which a teenage girl has her first orgasm the first time she has sex with a boy. To Annie, nothing could be more improbable. "I know everyone loved it," she says, "but I thought it was stupid."

Adam looks at her with mock horror. "You're insane."

"Maybe," she says. She likes Adam, and she is interested enough in the conversation to forget her unease in group settings, and to forget she hates baseball, and to half-forget Madeline. She is also aware that Adam is attracted to her; in a detached way, she enjoys the idea of being attractive. It is somehow easier to enjoy the conversation *because* she is not attracted to him.

It is the third inning, then the fifth inning, and then Annie needs to pee, desperately. The line for the women's bathroom is long and she wanders to the bathroom on the lower level, where the line is equally long. She waits, pees, and examines her reflection in the watery mirror over the sink. Her cheeks are flushed, bordering on red, and her hair has turned wavy in the heat. She looks happy, intriguing, maybe even pretty. "It's you," she says, to her reflection. Because, yes, she has been drinking. But also because it seems like not a terrible thing.

She leaves the bathroom, climbs the stairs to the third tier, and stops at a concession stand for what she decides will be her last beer. She is in line for a minute before she notices Madeline and Darby just a few feet ahead of her, their backs turned. Madeline reaches over and slides a finger beneath the strap of Darby's tank top, untwisting it. It is a small gesture — a *tiny* gesture — but it is all Annie needs to see. A kid at the back of the line starts howling, and Madeline turns to look at him. "Hey," she says to Annie. "Why

125

are you all the way back there?"

"Join us," Darby says.

"Actually," Annie says, "I just remembered I left my wallet under my seat." A lie: she does not own a wallet.

"We'll buy your beer or food or whatever," Madeline says.

"That's okay." Annie backs out of the line. "I should probably stop drinking, anyway."

She returns to her seat.

"You're back," Adam says. "You missed everything."

"Really?" Annie glances at the scoreboard, which reads zero to zero.

"No," Adam says.

They watch the field. A player in a red jersey is at bat. On the second pitch, he swings, and there is a cracking sound, and the ball soars over the field, into the stands. Everyone around them leaps to their feet, screaming and cheering and seeming wildly, stupidly enthusiastic. Annie remains seated.

After a minute, Adam sits down. He smiles. "You seem underwhelmed."

"I am."

He looks at her in a prolonged way—in a way no one ever looks at her—and she looks back until he leans over and kisses her. She lets him because, she thinks, maybe it will be different. Maybe she will feel something other than mild discomfort and boredom. But Adam's mouth is just a mouth, and it tastes like a hot dog. The kiss is brief, barely a kiss, and then he pulls away. He looks mortified. "Sorry," he says. "Should I not have done that?"

"No," Annie says, "I mean—"

"You are *totally* not into it," he says. "I'm *really* sorry."

"It's fine," Annie says. "Really." She is suddenly aware of the sweat pooling beneath her arms, of the rush of white noise in her ear. She is aware of the general wrongness of being here, next to a perfectly nice guy, watching a baseball game. She stands, climbs over a dozen sets of legs, and moves to the nearest stairway, down two flights of stairs, and out of the stadium. At the Metro entrance, she steps on the escalator, descends into the station, and passes through the turnstiles. The platform is crowded, and the board that supposedly displays the wait time is blank. She stares at the hexagon-shaped floor tiles. A train eventually arrives, and she steps into the car.

The air conditioning in the Metro car is broken. The train brakes and coasts forward, brakes and coasts forward. Annie feels nauseous almost immediately. A few feet away, a teenage girl in a jean shirt, jean shorts, and gleaming white sneakers applies lip liner, using the window as a mirror. After six or seven stops, Annie is on the verge of vomiting. She gets off at the next station, well before her stop, and emerges onto the street, walking for several blocks in a neighborhood dense with bars and restaurants before she recognizes the coffee shop where she ran into Madeline. She turns right at the Giant and finds herself in the same block as the dog park. At the entrance, she sees a young black guy in track pants and a t-shirt, crouched on the ground, pouring water from a bottle into a bowl. A white dog stands next to him, panting.

Annie remains outside the park and loops her fingers through the chain-link fence. Inside, there is a boxer and a border collie and a yellow lab and a pit bull mix, all doing the dog equivalent of milling around, waiting. She watches as they nudge at the gravel with their noses. She watches as a man scoops up a tennis ball and launches it across the park, three dogs racing after it. She watches as the border collie ignores the tennis ball. Instead, it runs in circles.

GROCERY SHOPPING

Sailing across Food Lion's gleaming floors,
she steers the prow of her steel-caged cart
away from aisles of items she knows by rote

toward those once deemed too rich, too fat.
Everything falls into the cart's mesh mouth—
deviled cakes sealed in cling wrap,

tubs of caramel corn, Nestle Combo-Packs
of ice-cream drumsticks poured into
Butterfinger-dipped cones. In the cool clutch

of air-conditioning, anonymity abounds,
each patron intent on their own hoard.
No one's pity plucks apart her skin

as if concern alone might cure the tumor
deep within. No one pries with paring knives,
blind to the way her responses spool

like flensed fat from a still-warm corpse.
No one weighs her down with tales
of those who beat the odds—

a husband's mother's neighbor
or some distant relative illusory as smog
blown out to sea. When her turn

at the register comes, the cashier says,
Have a nice day, already turning to the next
in line, grabbing something else to scan.

A.M. BRANDT

THE WAY WITH STUDENTS

We're sitting around the circle
like we do and I am being the me
they know and the me they don't.
Most days I live in terror of saying anything
that rises above my meaning.
Inside the room there is another sky
and sometimes it appears
unbroken, but the truth is it is
broken, even though I want us all
under it together, invisible, caught
on this side of presage, like a light falling
all of a kind. Someone desires leaves
through a bedroom window, someone
feels the walls for a switch, someone else
grabs a knife. There are whole days
moving out of the valley toward a wide slope
where anything might happen.
When I come home, the roses I never liked
have grown leggy and wild. My daughter
runs and whoops in green circles singing *poetry*
poetry is the death of all of us.
And the feral cat, usually so elusive, moves
through the boxwoods, lifting her face to me,
her body a shapely code, her voice barely there.

SEAFARING

My son holds his newborn, and vents unfasten,
releasing a power that smashes time's arrangement.

Remnants of my past breathe down my neck,
linger, then splinter. The floor plummets

and I'm between falling and diving, stretching
my fragile habitat through dense meadows

of underwater grasslands and oceanic currents.
Along coral reefs, I swim with sea horses.

An enclave opens, the inevitable.
I'm an ancient ship builder, assembling

and fastening planks of wood together,
paving the way for voyage. Swallowing

only light, I float to the rim of the sea
and send a message to my son—

your pearl of the world is born—I pray
to consequences that I'm an eternal sketch

on what lies ahead, his belief in our blood
and in the ways of water.

*"A very serious drinker," he said and flagged down
the bartender for another vodka-tonic.*

THE DEVIL IS BEATING HIS WIFE

Inevitable that it started on a porch, it being Clemson and the '80s and the lush red middle of a Carolina autumn. And though it was the porch of our own house, we should not have been there, neither Lazarus nor I. Where we should have been was a half-mile into campus, in a sad little room with walls the color of regurgitated oatmeal, where a Southern Lit professor was waiting to tell us about a Faulkner novel neither of us had bothered to buy. Our class was called "The Old South" and, since attending its opener, Laz and I had skipped all subsequent gatherings. The sweet old guy's mythology, while riveting, lacked traction. We could not suffer it.

It was this kind of indifference that made graduation in the spring increasingly unlikely. But, on the bright side, it was because we forgot "The Old South" that we were positioned on the porch just after sunrise to hear the screen door slam and see Joe, our longtime roommate, stumble out of the house looking stuck somewhere between a nightmare and a punchline. Joe was shirtless and had used duct tape to wrap his hands and knees in strips of tire. He made for an ambiguous beast, pitiful but not yet robbed of pride.

"Behold," said Laz, lit Philly fixed in the corner of his smirk. "Our resident deep-fried Romeo."

"Stay put!" croaked Joe and without looking at either of us lowered himself into the stance of a dog and crawled off the porch.

Like two men who've wandered into the same dream, Laz and I stood up and watched Joe use his jimmy-rigged paws to advance across the yard and onto the dirty pavement of Boudreaux boulevard.

"It's Tuesday," observed Laz. "Doesn't he have his Milton class at nine?"

I said nothing. For one, like Laz, I knew that whatever this was had something to do with Katie, Joe's longtime girl. On a deeper level, though, recent events had inclined me to silence. I'd seen a striped tabby stray named Penny appear in our window three days after we found her dead in the street and buried her. I'd seen a woman with bone-white hair run naked down the block at dawn crying, "Fill me! Fill me! Fill me!" And, two nights ago, I'd seen a black Cadillac, no driver, circle our street while a blood moon hung like an iced plum in the night sky.

It's true I came to Clemson a privileged hick with answers for everything, but the wild and difficult poetry of our senior year had worn me down and shut me up.

"White boys and their women," said Laz, waving his long black finger in my face and tisking out a tongue-cadence like some disapproving parent. "Are y'all not yet weary of this ancient cycle?"

After several moments of us just standing there, and Joe scrambling down Boudreaux, and the sweetness of our porch conspiring with the crunchy red leaves scattered across the lawn as if all was still lovely and ordained, I maintained my vow of silence but took off after Joe, catching him just before he turned left on Sarkey. Laz slapped his thighs and said, "By the hand of a God I no longer believe in, I swear it's time for something new!" With fierce reluctance, he followed.

"Hold up," I said, crouching in front of Joe and grabbing him by his shoulders.

Already sweat had bubbled in little pods across Joe's back. His face was cough-syrup purple and licked with dust. I didn't like what I was seeing: a broken man on a bad quest, all nightmare and no punchline, once you got up close. Glass half full, however, his paws were holding up just fine.

"Move!" Joe grunted, writhing in all directions against my grip.

"Speak," I replied. "Tell me what's going on here."

"I'll tell you what's going on," said Laz, the only one not breathing hard. "He's lost his girl and this is him winning her back. Joe, old buddy, have you considered a phone call? I bet Katie would appreciate that. Or how about a handwritten letter with a nice line from Yeats?"

I had dug my hands into Joe's shoulders and sprawled out so as to smother him with my full weight. He wasn't going anywhere but had yet to come around an acceptance of that reality.

"Move!" he screamed and continued pressing into me.

Laz lit a new cigar and said, "If self-flagellation is what you're after, I have a Civil War documentary back at the house. We can watch it together and I'll remind you what thieving ugly shits your people have been these last three centuries."

Joe didn't answer. He persisted. The sharp scratching on pavement, the unified throb of so many sunlit muscles: you knew it was noble even as you knew it was pointless. All I had to do was lean on him. And all Laz could do was watch my leaning until, after mustering one final torque, Joe's arms buckled and he collapsed.

"Enough," I said.

"That's right. Enough," Laz echoed. "Come home and I'll buy you a box of that beer you like."

Twice Joe tried to raise himself up. Both times I pinned him back to the ground. Following that he thrashed his head from side to side, ramming at empty air until his skull cracked against the pavement. A gash opened up above his left eye and a red rope descended through sweat and dust and sunlight. Joe used his forearm to wipe it and left a crimson smear across his forehead like some antique painted warrior.

"This is pointless," I said. "What's your goal here?"

"What's yours?" growled Joe.

Laz laughed and, approaching us, patted Joe between the shoulder blades. I momentarily relaxed my grip. Laz said, "Joe, you ever read Camus's thing on Sisyphus? How when you look at him pushing that boulder, you have to imagine—"

On "imagine," Joe exploded off the pavement and drove his head into the slack center of my gut. Down I went. Down Laz went too, though he hadn't even been touched. By the time we found our feet, Joe was gone, clear around the corner for Sarkey.

"Come on!" I said, motioning Laz back to the house. "Plan B."

"Plan B?" Laz mocked.

"Please," I said.

"What in the hell," Laz said and did not contain his disgust. "Is Plan B."

Plan B was this: we'd use the moped to shoot ahead of Joe and set up at what I called "checkpoints." Plan B was walking with a man you could not stop. Sometime between getting knocked on my ass and returning to our house, I had completed the rough calculations.

"Our boy's moving at two miles an hour," I said. "If it's six miles to Katie's place, we'll set up once at Freedie's. Again at The Recovery Room. And a final time at Old Son's. That's three legs to home."

I watched Laz run the logistics in his head. Truth is, it worked out, right down to the three bars breaking Joe's journey into three equal stretches.

"That's the dumbest thing I've ever heard," Laz said. "I want nothing to do with this scheme. I'd rather sit on this porch and hit each of my toes with a claw hammer."

But when I revved the moped and started out of the driveway, Laz hopped on.

"For the record," Laz said, as we sped down Boudreaux. "I'd rather be reading Faulkner."

My math was off. We drank at Freedie's for two hours with no sign of Joe. Which was fine by us. Killing time with talk and booze was exactly what we'd be doing back at Boudreaux.

"Tell me what I'm missing about your kind," said Laz, who already had a steady buzz going. "Tell me a single thing to redeem this pitiful endeavor."

I did not know and would not ask what Laz meant by my "kind." There was no point. It could've meant region, since both Joe and I were from Carolina whereas Laz hailed from somewhere in Alabama. Or, it could've meant race, since Laz was black and Joe and I were white. It even could've referred to sexuality, since both Joe and I would gladly drink the bathwater of the women we loved and Laz was, by his own admission, asexual. But likely what it meant was all three of those distinctions and ten more we didn't even know existed. Because that was Laz's gift—exiling himself from whatever categories the too-tidy South could conjure up.

"Okay," I said. "Atonement."

"Atonement?" Laz said and was smirking as if speaking with a child who received a C-minus in comprehension. "And when Katie opens her door and looks down on his sorry ass, what will atonement get him?"

"If it works, she'll think he's sorry. If it really works, she'll take him back."

This drew a laugh from Laz. He killed his vodka-tonic in one large gulp and readjusted his little black baron fedora. It's worth noting that Laz extended his pilgrim status straight into the aesthetical realm. He wore black, regardless of the occasion. Black shirt, black jeans, black boots, and that black fedora, which sat askew on his head like a thing poached from John Dillinger's dumpster. His attire, so dark and loose and strange, made it impossible to tell, even close up, if he was male or female, heavy metal or homeless. To further dislodge him from what he often called "the teeming mass of humanity," Laz routinely shaved every inch of his body, including his scalp and his eyebrows. No one, not even Joe and I, who had roomed with Laz since freshman year, knew what to make of him, other than the plain fact that he was as alone as any one person could be, struck from the map of all conceivable categories, and therefore able to critique our kind or any other kind with relative impunity.

"I know a bit about atonement," Laz said.

"Is that right?"

"My mother was Baptist," he said. "Have I ever told you that?"

He had not and I admitted as much. I finished the drink in front me and realized that I, too, was nursing a nice fog.

"She was," Laz continued. "A very serious Baptist, actually. And do you know what my father was?"

"What?"

"A very serious drinker," he said and flagged down the bartender for another vodka-tonic. When his drink arrived, he continued: "And when my old man had been drinking, he did not exercise what you would call good judgement. After hitting the bars, he would come home, not mean or abusive, but just very late and very drunk. And do you know what my mother would do when he came home?"

"What?"

"She would bolt the door shut and make my father enter the house through the doggy door."

"You're kidding."

"I'm not," Laz said. "And my father, not a small man, would do it. It became a kind of ritual for them. Her standing there in the hall like some kind of bronze statue of a martyr. And him grunting loud enough to wake half the neighborhood and busting half the muscles in his back squeezing through that door."

"That's wild," I said and tried to envision my own father doing such a thing. I could not.

"But get this," Laz replied. "I remember this one time when it happened, and I got out of bed, and I snuck over to the top of the stairs where I could watch. And my father, who was that night especially hammered, could only make it halfway through the doggy door. He had worked his head, shoulders, and chest through, but his gut had gotten caught and he was too drunk and too tired to yank it all the way through."

"So what did he do?"

"He looked up at my mom and said, 'Why do you do this to me, Fran? Does it make you hot to see me hurt like this?' And from the top of the stairs I watched my mother do a strange thing. I watched her walk over to where he was stuck, slip out of her panties, lift her nightgown over her hips, and lower her bare bottom directly onto his face. And I watched as my old man smiled and used to his tongue to—"

"Ugh," I muttered. "No more. Why tell me this?"

"Because," Laz said. "If that's atonement, you can keep it. I don't believe in it. I need something new."

"No disrespect to your parents, Laz, but this is different. Joe loves Katie. If this is his way of showing it, I'm in no position to judge."

"*Love*," Laz said, ridding his mouth of the word like it was an especially lowly form of fungal matter.

"Yes," I said. "Love. It's a thing. You should try it sometime."

"Love," Laz continued. "Is like the elephant and the blind men. Surely you, an English major and a runaway Presbyterian, are familiar with that parable?"

"No," I admitted. "I'm not."

"An elephant comes to town," Laz said. "Three men, all blind since birth, approach the great beast. One grabs it by the ear and says to his friends, 'I finally know what an elephant is! It is soft and floppy like a blanket.' When the second blind man hears this, he becomes upset. You see, the second blind man is holding the elephant by its leg. 'You are a liar!' he screams. 'I am touching the elephant now and it is big and sturdy like a tree.' The first and second blind man begin to fight and become so engrossed in their argument that they cannot hear the third blind man, who is holding the elephant by his tail and swearing by heaven and earth that elephants are thin, stick-like creatures. That, young man, is love."

"I get it," I said. "It's a nice parable."

"And that's a nice blind man," Laz replied and pointed out of the bar's window and down towards the street. It was Joe.

Joe refused to come in. Committed to his new form, he refused to even sit up while we spoke to him. The best we got was a nod or shake.

"You ready to go home and get that beer?" I said.

Shake.

"You ready to tell us what this is all about?"

Shake.

"Well, you look like shit," said Laz. "At least let us get you some water."

Joe, meeting our eyes for what might have been the first time that day, wiped the sweat from his eyes and nodded.

Laz ducked into the pharmacy and returned with a bottle of water, a blue plastic bowl, and a tube of sunscreen. After Laz had set the bowl on the pavement and filled it with water, Joe plunged his face into it and attacked the liquid with a desperate series of gulps. While Laz used a napkin to clean the cut above his eye, I opened the sunscreen and applied it generously to Joe's back and arms and calves, all of which were already darkening with the pink beginning of a bad burn.

When Joe had finished drinking and looked apt to leave, I knelt beside him and said, "If you're heading to Katie's, wouldn't a moped get you there a little quicker?"

"It would," Joe said, using his teeth to adjust the tire strapped to his left hand. "But it would also miss the point."

Sensing that we'd lose him at any moment, I said, "But what's the point, Joe?"

"If I make to Katie's place, you'll see," he said.

Then he was gone. We lingered for a while to watch him go. People on the sidewalk jumped back as he crawled past. A little girl dropped her lollipop and cried. Then a fat and hateful-looking white man with a patchy beard and a camouflage hat pulled up in a truck and began yelling something at Joe. From the back of this angry chub's vehicle waved the largest Confederate flag I'd ever seen in my life. The flag dwarfed the truck. Whatever this man was yelling, Joe wasn't responding. And, failing to get his desired response, Flag Boy chucked a bottle of dip-spit at Joe's head. The bottle struck him squarely, spilling its brown slime across Joe's neck and back. Flag Boy then slapped his hand on the side of his truck and laughed as if the funniest joke in the world had just been made just for him. Then he threw something else, something that made a sharp, metallic clank when it hit the pavement in front of Joe's face. It sounded like a wrench.

"'Old South' my ass," I said. "Let's drag that racist asshole out of his truck and kick his teeth in."

"That," Laz said, "would miss the point."

After a brief debate, we left Joe there and took back roads to The Recovery Room.

As at Freedie's, we ordered drinks at The Recovery Room and resumed our talk. We killed a good half hour discussing strategies for bullshitting our way through Southern Lit. Laz happened to know a guy who knew his Faulkner. I happened to know our old professor's favorite bourbon. Failure did not concern us.

Following that, we sat for a while and said nothing, just watched the television above the bar, which was showing one of those daytime talk shows where couples who hate each other publicly receive the results of paternity tests. We watched a young white man with shitty teeth and neck tattoos get confirmation that he was not the father of the child in question. The mother wept into her own arms. The man jumped up and down, pumping his fists in celebration, as if he had just won the lottery.

"I'm free!" the man screamed and extended not one but two stiff middle fingers at the weeping woman, his non-wife, non-mother-of-his-child. "From here on out, I don't want to hear shit

141

about that baby!"

"Well," said Laz. "If that's not emblematic of our present state of affairs, I don't know what is."

I laughed and, sensing the talk was about to circle back to Joe, made up my mind to ask a question I'd been sitting on ever since I met Lazarus. I said, "Hey, Laz, what are you going to do after graduation?"

Laz glared at me for asking this. It was the kind of look you gave someone for farting in a hot car.

"Why are you asking?" he said.

"Because I'm genuinely curious," I said. "I always have been."

Laz nodded, apparently accepting this as a valid motivation. Then he smiled widely and said, "I think I'll hang myself from the Centennial Oak. Possibly with a quote from Baldwin stapled to my chest."

"Stop," I said. "Be serious. What are your plans?"

"Who knows?" he said and shrugged. "Maybe I'll join the winos down in Easley. Failing that, I could always teach high school English. What about you?"

"I don't know," I said because, for me, there was nothing on earth more true.

"Think you'll marry that girl you're always bringing back to the house? The rich white one with the nice teeth and the fat can?"

I didn't deign to answer this. Laz knew Madison's name, just as he knew that I had worked doubles at Nick's Tavern last summer to save up for an engagement ring. Laz being Laz, he probably even knew that the ring was sitting in my sock drawer, just waiting around, like Madison herself, for me to make up my mind.

"Let me ask you something," I said, figuring it was as good a time as ever to fire off one more thing I'd always been curious about.

"Shoot," said Laz.

"You really don't believe in anything?"

"Nope."

"What does that make you? Some kind of nihilist or something?"

"Don't know, don't care."

"And you plan to spend your entire life alone?"

"That's right."

Laz's certainty at that moment — and, to be clear, Laz never seemed anything less than certain — reminded me of something he had once said in American literature class. Our professor, a widely published young lady who had recently arrived in Clemon by way of southern California, put Laz on the spot by asking him what he thought about racial relations in the New South. Everyone in the room, which is to say seventeen white people and one Asian-American, looked at Laz and waited for his response. What he said when he finally decided to speak was this: "When exactly did this new South arrive?"

Our professor, who, while out in Southern California, had done extensive research on civil rights and African-American literature, provided Laz with a timeline of black achievements and legislative breakthroughs. Laz let her finish before he started laughing. "Who knew?" was his response. The professor continued her lecture and, as far as I can recall, never again called on Laz.

And yet, there in The Recovery Room, we seemed to be gaining ground.

"What happened to you?" I said. "Have you always been this way?"

"I believed in something once," said Laz. "His name was Homer."

"Well," I said. "Tell me about Homer."

"He was an old thirty-buck mutt we rescued," said Laz. "I must have been about seven or eight years old when we got him. And I took old Homer everywhere with me. Even took him in bed until Mama found ticks in the sheets and exiled Homer to our sorry excuse for a backyard."

"What else?" I said. "Keep going."

Such vulnerability from Laz was rare. In our years of living together, he'd dropped his guard less than a dozen times. With respect to information on his past, I would push him as far as he would go.

"Let's see," Laz said and could not hide his smile. "Homer had a limp. He had it when we got him. Never knew why. Probably his previous owner was some mouthbreather who kicked him around for fun. He'd try his best to run with you but he never could keep up. You'd look over your shoulder and see him hoofing it like the devil was on his heels."

Something was changing in Laz's face and in his voice. I did not like where things were heading but lacked the heart to stop him.

Laz continued: "I was coming home one night. I'd been out nightswimming. Homer was right behind me. At least I thought he was. And I had almost made it my house when I heard a sound too awful to tell. I thought someone had fired a gun. It was that loud. When I turned around, I saw this car speeding off. There's a stop sign at the end of our street and they blew right through it. Just a pair of tail lights fading off into the night."

Laz was holding the bar with both hands and wincing, like a fighter squinting into an impending blow. And yet, he looked as if he was going to continue with the story, which I did not want him to do.

"That's enough," I said. "I understand."

"Then I saw Homer," he said. "He was smeared across the street. The entire back half of his body had been crushed and more blood than I'd ever seen was spreading like rain across the pavement."

"Okay," I repeated. "Enough."

"Hold on, though, because here's the point. Homer kept on coming. He was dead and didn't even know it, but his eyes were locked on me and his front legs were scrambling like there was still a chance. And I'll never forget that. Homer, smeared across the street, but right up to the end fighting his way back home."

"Damn, Laz."

"Exactly."

I was going to say something dumb and insensitive, something like "I can see why you don't believe in shit. If I had your past, I wouldn't believe in shit, either." But I never got the chance. A sound was coming from outside, the swelling volume of which pulled us from our conversation. It was the sound of many feet moving at once and a flood of unfamiliar voices all swirling together. We looked outside and saw Joe. He was no longer alone.

The situation outside was absurd. In addition to the two dozen followers who had formed in a loose ring around Joe, there was a news crew, a street-corner preacher, and some girl with a nose-ring holding up a hand-painted sign that read 'MEAT IS MURDER!' A blonde reporter was talking into her cameras, periodically motioning back at Joe. The street preacher was distributing small blue pamphlets to anyone who'd have them, while the girl with the sign was thrashing around behind the reporters, screaming about an upcoming bill. I also noticed Flag Boy riding high in his truck. He'd been joined by a couple of equally large and angry-looking white dudes, all of whom were having a good laugh over Joe's pain.

Our first minute with Joe was spent stripping him of the various accessories he'd accumulated since our last checkpoint. Two flags, one Clemson and the other Palmetto, had been draped over his neck. His back was plastered with stickers, some for indie bands and some for local politicians. All four pockets of his jeans were stuffed full with takeout menus and business cards.

"You've developed quite a following," I said, peeling a "Bird Dog's BBQ" sticker off Joe's ribcage.

As if he had not noticed until that very moment, Joe glanced at the crowd and shrugged.

145

"How are you holding up?" I asked.

Nod.

"Let's get some food in you before this next leg," I said. "How's that sound?"

Shake.

"Then at least drink some water," I said, filling the blue bowl with water and sliding it under Joe's face.

Joe drank. Meanwhile, the blonde reporter approached us. She was short and, too many years past pretty, had buried her smiling face beneath about a quarter-pound of make-up.

"Excuse me, gentlemen," she said, arranging herself beside us while still smiling into the camera. "You seem to be acquainted with this man. Can you speak towards his purpose? Can you tell us why he's doing this?"

"No," I said, swatting her microphone away as if it were a gnat that had forgotten its place.

Entirely unfazed, the blonde continued: "It's been suggested that this is some kind of statement. Is it related to the racial issues in upcoming election? Is it a symbol of Senator Wilson's refusal to — "

"I said no!" I yelled. "Now get back!"

The rest of the crowd drew back. The blonde, however, remained. "How do you two know 'The Crawler'?" she said. "Can you at least tell us that much?"

"'The Crawler'?" Laz said, looking along with me into the blonde's television-tight eyes.

"Yes," she said. "That's what people are calling him."

Before we could make a decision regarding the most diplomatic way to drive back the blonde and the rest of the clingers, a fight broke out between the girl with the nose-ring and a woman who must have weighed three hundred pounds. The large woman was attempting to rip the sign out of the girl's hands, screaming as she did something about God commanding men to subdue animals. The girl with the nose-ring was landing mean left hooks onto the woman's quivering jowls. Flag Boy, who had a can of beer in his hand, whooped and laid on the horn. When the camera swung to capture the brawl, we led Joe around the corner and into an alley.

"Halfway home," I said, dabbing at the cut above his eye, which had stopped bleeding but was still glistening in its freshness. "How you feeling?"

"Strong," said Joe and did not resist me prying bits of broken glass and pebbles out of his paws.

"Good," I said. "Your entourage isn't slowing your pace, are they?"

"They won't be around much longer," said Joe, looking up at the sky. "The Devil's about to beat his wife."

We looked up. Sure enough, with the sun shining fat and yellow in the middle of the blue sky, warm drops of rain began splattering the ground around us. Harder than I knew rain could fall, it came from the sky in buckets and drenched everything in sight. The news crew jumped into their van. The crowd either ducked into The Recovery Room or took off running down the street. We sat there together in the alley and let it soak our faces and hair and bodies. We squinted upwards, in awe of that rare conspiracy between sun and storm.

Eventually, Joe began to move.

"Onward and upward," Laz said flatly and slapped Joe on the ass as he crawled by.

Noticeably slower, Joe moved out of the alley and made his way down Saint Mark's. We settled our tab with The Recovery Room and ran through the rain for the moped. We had revved it and nearly pulled off when a face appeared before us.

"Let me just ask you one question," said this new face, dripping wet and spitting water.

Laz and I studied the figure. It took us a moment to place him. We did, though, eventually. It was the street preacher, his blue pamphlets a pulpy bouquet stuffed down into a tightly clenched fist.

"Who do you believe can deliver you from this present hell?" he screamed.

"Out of our way!" I said, whipping the moped to the left.

But the preacher jumped with us, grabbing the handlebars and planting his feet.

"You could die tonight, son!" he shouted. "And if you did, do you believe you'd gain access to the new heaven and the new earth? Don't you want access, son?"

"Keep your access!" Laz replied and I gave the moped gas.

The moped jumped forward. I don't know if the bike struck him or if he flung himself to avoid the collision, but the preacher went down. I do know this: as we sped down the wet road towards Saint Mark's, he was back on his feet and shouting, "Repent and believe! Repent and believe!"

It was still pouring when we got to Old Son's. Sully, the manager there, gave us each a towel and made us dry off before coming inside. Once we did, we took a booth with a good view of the street and started on the Beam. You could almost see Katie's house from the street outside the bar. She lived in a little yellow house up on the hill.

"Fuck belief," Laz said, once he was several whiskeys in and thoroughly drunk from all the day's drinks. "And fuck love. Love's not real. Throw love in with the other revisionist lies and social constructions. Burn all that shit to cinders. We're in here talking out of our asses, and Joe's out there killing himself for a bad joke."

"You're missing the point," I said.

"Suddenly there's a point to this story?" Laz said. "By all means, enlighten me."

"The point of belief is believing," I said. "The point is finding whatever keeps you from hanging yourself. The point is not truth, it's moving forward."

"Moving forward," Laz said and winked at me. "Boy, we're crushing that one down here, aren't we? But I've seen how belief plays itself out."

"Yeah?"

"Yeah," Laz said. "It's like this little fool I knew back in high school. He used to put rocks in his shoes then walk around."

"Rocks? Why rocks?"

"Said it was for Jesus."

"Ouch," I said. "But why? Why would Jesus want to hurt him?"

"You know, believe it or not, I asked him about that. But the son of a bitch would never give me a straight answer. I must've asked him a hundred times. After a while he'd just smile at me and, with this weird look in his eyes, say, 'At the center of love is death.'"

"That's deep," I admitted.

"About as deep as a man crawling across the county line for love."

"You're still missing the point."

"Tell me, then, General Pickett," Laz said, smirking. "What is the point?"

"The point is broken people need something to believe in. It doesn't matter what. Belief beats cynicism. It beats materialism. And it's a hell of a lot better than the shitshow out there."

Laz let out a series of disapproving tisks. Then he said, "The only thing your kind believes in is licking their own wounds. That must be a Southern thing. I spent a summer in Colorado. The men out there eat sushi and climb mountains. You don't see anyone scraping pavement with their gut in the name of love."

"I don't buy that," I replied.

"Buy this," he said and from his pocket pulled two folded pieces of paper and slid them across the table. I opened them. They were letters, one from Katie to Joe and one from Joe to Katie.

"Found those when I was cleaning all those menus out of his pockets," said Laz.

"And?"

"Read them," said Laz.

149

I slid the letters back to Laz. A look of disappointment, even betrayal, flashed across his face.

"You not going to read them?" he said. "Hell of an English major you are."

"Why? What's the point?"

"We've been wondering this whole time what he did. It's all right there. Read it."

"Did he go somewhere he shouldn't have?"

"He did."

"Did he lie about it?"

"Somewhat."

"Did he swear to Katie, after the fact, that it meant nothing and will never happen again?"

"Basically."

"So what's to read? I get it. Hell, I've lived it."

"Live this," Laz muttered, unfolding the letter and scanning its contents for the line he had in mind.

"'Katie, please believe me,'" Laz read, doing his best impression of Joe's voice. "'Please believe me that nothing in this world could stop me from loving you. I am sorry for what I did, what I still do. I won't always be this way. Please forgive me while I am.'"

Laz paused and looked up. In his normal voice he said, "Those are Joe's words."

"So what?" I said.

"You ready for Katie's response?"

"I don't need to—"

"'I don't believe you,'" Laz continued over me, now high-pitched and imitating Katie. "'I think you are a liar. I think you've lied for so long you no longer know you're doing it. But I'll tell you what, if this is real, why don't you show me how sorry you are?'"

Laz refolded the letter and slid it in his pocket.

"I rest my case," said Laz. "If that's belief, then you can keep it. I need something new."

"I will keep it," I said.

"Why?"

"Because there's shit else going," I said. "And because if there was something new out there, we would have found it by now."

I watched Laz's face when I said this, expecting some kind of reaction. But Laz was neither looking at me nor listening to me. His gaze, widened and stuffed with something like concern, had cast itself towards the street. I whipped around and saw what was breaking Laz's heart. It broke mine too.

Joe was outside and he had been stopped and circled by Flag Boy and three of his friends. They were spitting beer onto his head and riding him like a horse. They were sticking their boots into his face. Then Joe said something. Whatever it was turned their violence serious. They started kicking Joe for real. One man connected with his ribs. Flag Boy smashed him in his teeth. Laz saw this too and but seemed to have entered into a realm beyond normal human emotion. In the very moment when he should've looked angry, he looked tranquil. His eyes had a thick, religious glaze, and he appeared to me a man under some kind of spell. And though no sound was coming out, his lips were moving, whispering something too soft to make out. Laz stood up from the table and slowly started towards the exit. I got up too and followed him.

"Laz," I said. "What's the plan here?"

He said nothing and kept walking. I sensed, then, that something new and terrible was about to happen.

"Laz!" I shouted and seized him by the arm, hoping to snap him out of his trance.

But Laz did not even look at me. With a strength that surprised me, he pried my hand off his arm and, still singing, marched out of the bar and towards Joe and the men.

Our presence startled Flag Boy and his crew. They stopped kicking Joe and looked at where we were standing, somewhat at me but mostly at Laz.

"What the hell are you supposed to be?" Flag Boy said and spit on the ground in Laz's general direction.

Laz did not respond. Instead, with great deliberation, he removed the black fedora from his head and placed it on the pavement. Then he removed his black shirt, folded it into a perfect square, and lay it beside the fedora. I struggled to process all that was happening. Joe was writhing down there on the pavement, bleeding from about five different places. The sky was still spitting grey sheets of rain. Flag Boy and his friends were alternating between talking shit to Joe and laughing at Laz. Then all of it, every component part of the crazy nightmare this day had become since we skipped our class to sit on the porch, was suddenly drowned out by what I saw on Laz's body, by what I saw on his skin.

I had never seen him with his shirt off and it was at that very moment that I realized why. Hundreds, and I mean *hundreds*, of scars covered his arms and his stomach and his chest. Some were flat and no bigger than a toothpick, but others were raised and closer in size to a pencil. I had never in my life seen anything like it. "Cutting" was not a word known or used at Clemson in the 1980's.

"You have one job, brother," Laz said to me, out of his spell and looking at Flag Boy with more rage than I had ever seen in a pair of human eyes.

"Anything," I said.

"Make sure you get Joe to Katie's."

I looked at Laz, and he nodded, and in that nod was more heart than the whole of Clemson combined. I knew there was no arguing with him. Had he asked me, I would've followed him into the fires of Hell.

"Can you do that?" Laz said.

"I can," I replied.

After that, Lazarus ran straight up to Flag Boy and drove his fist so hard into that man's face, that I could hear the crunch of nose bones from fifteen feet back. And if you think he stopped after that, you are wrong. With rain slamming down on everything, and blood leaking out of faces and mouths and hands, and me scooping Joe off the ground, and the whole world seeming at that moment to tremble and spin like a broken carousel, Laz kept punching and kicking and biting and screaming. For a moment, it did not matter that he was outnumbered. His fists were everywhere at once, dropping his enemies one after another.

Remembering my promise, I dragged Joe to the moped and revved it. Joe croaked something then, but his mouth was full of blood and his voice too faded to hear. It could have been "Go." Or, it could have been "No." I never asked. I kept my promise to Laz, hitting the gas and tearing out of there, away from Old Son's and up towards that yellow house on the hill.

I allowed myself, just once, to look back. I have regretted this ever since. Because what I saw was that Flag Boy and his friends had regained the advantage. They were holding Laz down and beating him, mercilessly. Even still, that is not what I remember. What I remember is how Laz was smiling like a mad saint. How, even as they continued to punch him, he grinned directly into the center of their devilish faces and was shouting something that sounded like, "Mine! Mine! Mine!"

I kept my word and got Joe to Katie's. After a little arguing and much weeping, she forgave him and, no shit, they have been blissed-out ever since. Meanwhile Laz's fate became a profound mystery that he himself would've delighted in. When he never showed up at Boudreaux, we went to Old Son's and Sully told us Laz was taken by ambulance to the hospital in Oconee. We drove there but were turned away by a team of nurses nearly icy in their professionalism. Then, for weeks, nothing. Laz never came back to Boudreaux. Neither did he come back to Clemson. And wherever he ended up, he did not feel inclined to call or write. We tried several times to look him up, but no one even knew his last name.

In time, we all forgot him. Graduated, left, settled, and sunk. Clemson became a place you returned to for football. Our old house on Boudreaux: torn down to make room for a shopping center. But, for a while there, I looked forward to Laz's second coming, waiting for the day we'd drag a box of beer out on the porch and roll back time to make sense of things. I'd sit in that room the color of regurgitated oatmeal and listen to our old watery-eyed prof carry on about the "Old South," and I'd think of the day I would tell Lazarus that he no longer fooled me. Because I had seen the light of his face in battle, and it was holy with truth and love, the face of a believer.

FINGERS WITHOUT HANDS

Forgive me if I am corn without
its husk, strings of you hanging
on but don't mistake yourself. I am
fine, you are not my water,

my soil. Nutrients pump through
my core, with or without. My hull
is gone, enticing a cruel
winter, a vicious storm, but I last. So, pick

apart my pieces raw. My roots
will remain sturdy. You cannot
stop the rain's wash, the full
coverage of my earth.

AS IT MUST BE

When I heard
your hushed voice on the phone from your room,
I lost my balance, the shift, how you'd begun
to cast off on your own,
other suns in your firmament.
We all must learn to navigate the world,
which lights in the night-sky to trust,
how to beat a path through the gales,
the doldrums of February.
When you were small we'd stand together
and I'd block the gusts for you.
I'd tell you how the seasons change,
where birds go at night,
why your mother and I were not together.
The first time you lied to me,
I staggered back
from the split in the ground, lost,
not knowing how I'd find a way back to you.
After days, when you looked at me,
I finally saw you were just sorting your way.
Now you must learn to suffer
the solitude of crowds,
find your own songs
to pull from the wind
as I learn to live without your voice
warming the room beside mine.
There will be others with whom

you'll storm the jagged walls of longing,
roaming the sky above the hills
not far from where I fought.
I will stay here and go on
planting my small trees,
listen for your voice
when you call across our days.
It is as it must be.

PILGRIMS

We inch and ache, arrive at the wreck,
and whisk to the waiting room
where Theo can be changed
and wander around
the vending machines, drinking fountains,
Missys' boutique display case.
Six months ago, at my last
appointment, he slept in the car seat.

Entering this morning
a red river of brake lights, perfect storm
of car crashes and road work, we hit
bumper-to-bumper rush hour
traffic with him strapped
in a dirty diaper.

An hour late, I settle in
with my clipboard's checklist of symptoms
across from a teenage girl
in a hoodie. Exhaust pipes spiraled
windy contrails along I-470,
wisps lifting off into sky cloud, snow cloud,
cypresses and junipers bowing
below the weight of their white cassocks.

Theo's cries reached a pitch
of pure hysteria.

Now I see him rapt, in jaw-dropped
amazement before the girl and her parents.
She lowers her hood and laughs,
displaying her baldness, her catheter,
her unspeakable smile.

I like watching the albino ferret at midnight walk
past me meditating on the porch as if I were
another piece of deck furniture.

BACK FROM ABROAD

homo viator (man the traveler)
— Gabriel Marcel

Or not. Isn't New Hampshire just another chapter of Abroad? You're as likely to find a welcome wagon here as a tumbril, or an Obama bandwagon. Yankee self-reliance run amok? You can live twenty years next to somebody before you exchange a greeting. New Hampshire is old men on motorcycles with do-rags for helmets and army surplus shovels to scrape off road kill and say they bagged it. It's guys with sawed-off shotguns in freezing cold bulrushes waiting to fill Osama Bin Canard's backside with buckshot. New Hampshire is where bootstraps ride up to become indistinguishable from chin straps. Half of the guys in this *neighborhood*—a misnomer, actually, let's call it the *area* within your field of vision from the four corners of your yard—can build a house from the ground up. I'm the only guy without a pickup, a snowplow or blower, a sit-down mower, and a gun. Not that I take pride in any of that—except the un-gun.

Our coffee beans are from Kenya and our neighbors' are from Walmart. They still eat "Freedom fries" and see us as exiles from the People's Republic of Cambridge; we are that and more—we must be curmudgeons . . . because, ironically, *we prefer it here.* Most of my criticisms are some version of jealousy. A pickup would make life here much easier, if I could afford one. But I like seeing deer tracks in the early morning snow on the driveway. I like the peepers dueling it out with the crickets. I like watching the albino ferret at midnight walk past me meditating on the porch as if I were another piece of deck furniture, and I like watching the woodchuck undulate and hump his way to his hole under the garage as if he learned to run in a woodchuck hospice. And the green bird this morning who took me for either St. Francis or a garden gnome and alighted on my cap — the green one with a single red star that Ellen brought back from China for me.

If Buddy Holley et al. could have sat in the Adirondacks on my deck and heard the neighbor's chickens clucking, they would have drummed up rock and roll much sooner. And when Robt. Johnson took off for that mysterious interlude I can assure you that he was here at the moment the neighbors took the rooster away after they cooked the fattest mama hen, Mr. Rooster watching the plucking and hours later sensing the sun before it rose, knowing he was next, knowing just as sadly that his song had been reduced to cockadoodledoo or cucurrucucu — isn't that the blues? Robt. Johnson saw it all, heard every thing that preceded the sizzle and fry that he cooked up, rendered it his.

Nostalgia — it sounds like a disease; today my *pied á terre* is *la boue*. And I wallow. I'm watching the beautiful *Cinema Paradiso* for the second time, and there's the astonishing screen kiss, banned by the local sacerdote. It's so un-porn, nostalgia embodied, and reminds me of Warhol's apothegm: "Sex is just nostalgia for sex." The old projectionist, Alfredo, warns the young artist/cineaste, "Don't give in to nostalgia." But no, Alfredo, *mai*! Alfredo, *mai*! And in the end, the gray-haired cineaste watches a montage of kisses cut from all the films when he was a kid. And it's another version of that that I'm doing now — nostalgizing, in the kitchen under 18th century beams — CSNY on the radio — "Ships on the ocean, free and easy" carry me back to Senegal in 1970, the bougainvillea on the balcony of my paramour/spy's apartment looking over the *terrain vague* where the lepers played soccer on something like skateboards, in turn overlooked by the Lebanese landlord's telescope, Trina's shutters open, her exchange for free tenancy, CSNY doing the same songs on her primitive stereo. I'm cooking now and it has to be something infused with nostalgia — banana bread or maybe a quick trip to a specialty store that might have a tin of Clément-Faugier *crème de marrons*; I think I've seen, in Shaw's or Market Basket, *crème fraiche*. Mix them. Devour it.

Devouring a delicious almond croissant at Lil's Café in Kittery, I'm looking at a young man with a surprising resemblance to me at twenty-one, embarking for Senegal. He wears white shorts over white knee-breeches, the skin of his left leg below the knee obliterated by a gangrenous tattoo. I write these lines, look up, and he is gone, leaving me to ponder how times and fashion have changed, and *"plus ça . . ."* what remains is just a sense of goneness, reminding me of Simone de Beauvoir on her deathbed waxing nostalgic while simultaneously outraged by death — such a waste. All that beautiful personal experience *écrasé*. It makes one wish/pray for a Chardinesque vision of collective consciousness, not wasted but *recherché*, a noosphere surrounding the planet, beauty condensing and falling on us like oobleck — Bartholomews, all of us, hoping for something besides death to rain down. In Seuss' book, all one has to do is say "I'm sorry," and *it* goes away. *Beauty*? Or *death*? The choice perhaps made for you.

I've chosen a large latte, despite the outrageous price, to kickstart this morning, feeling tired, which makes me recall the Persian phrase, *kha-sté na-baw-shid*, which means "Don't be tired," but it is used to encourage a performer or to goad or console an exasperated teacher, which I was during a short stint in Iran — hardly worth rambling about — where I taught the *sarbaszes* — conscripted soldiers. "*Kha-sté na-baw-shid*" — it came from all corners of the box of a room after I refused to join the cluster-fuck of Mr. Gnademy when the lights went out in the classroom inside the hangar when a cat fell into the generator of the intelligence coordinating facility of the Shah's Imperial Iranian Air Force. And when, an hour later, the lights came back on and I was teaching the 'air-ladies', I admonished Ms. Nadimy for copping a feel of Ms. Parvaneh Hossein-Zadeh's lovely breast, and because they understood that the rebuke was a veiled expression of jealousy, they told me *not to be tired* and laughed like hell because my chastisement: "Kuchikoo, Ms. Nadimy?" in Farsi meant "Little mountain," which everybody understood as a metaphor for the gorgeous breast of Ms. Parvaneh Hossein-Zadeh, whose given name meant "butterfly."

And I'm thinking, at this outdoor table at Lil's, that if I were a butterfly, this would be the page I would debut on, as a Monarch stretches its wings to live up to its name and alights on a flower — for good reason: these are the finest flowers in Kittery, though the range of a Monarch is thousands of miles, but it's like Kierkegaard said — *stop and smell the roses,* and I do, but it doesn't deter me from thinking that Kierkegaard had too many vowels in his name, then deciding instead that there are too many consonants, and later that maybe he had it just right, and I'm like Goldilox and the three bagels, though Kierkegaard had only doubles on Ks, Es, and As, so it is a false comparison, "just my imagination, *runnin* away with me," and the *with* there implies control rather than companionship, like me and my shadow, or wait — that actually implies both, and sometimes I can't wait for night; feeling, like the Monarch, that in a garden like this, who needs imagination?

Don't be tired, *Parvaneh.*

Time-out for Finality

Hannah Arendt, in an obituary, let Heidegger off the Nazi-hook, likening him to Greek philosopher Thales, who fell into a well while gazing at the stars. He was probably singing — she did not add — "Throw the Jew down the well." (*pace* Borat — Sasha Baron Cohen)

Heidegger got planted in a Catholic cemetery, his last wish. Go figure.

Henry Miller:	"Old age is an obscene calamity."
J. P. Sartre:	"Death is an outrage."
S. de Beauvoir:	"Death is an intrusion, an abomination."

Homo viator
could not
agree more.

I wonder now, so many years later, if the answer to an editor's question on this piece, *"What was at stake?"* was vision—*a* vision. Let me explain. Shortly before embarking for Senegal in '68 I attended—leerily, cynically—a "happening." I don't remember what happened. It did not leave me enlightened. I'm sure almost nothing happened. But I remember it as a surprisingly positive experience, and though I thought nothing of it *in media res*, I realize now that it was an affirmation of the spark of human invention that coalesces out of communion, out of simply being—together, which was somewhere between BEING and NOTHINGNESS: it was decidedly *un*existential, seemingly inauthentic conformism which incited the communes of the 70s, so many people, including myself, living in group houses. But I did not foresee that. My path was decidedly existential. It was, as Mailer wrote in "The White Negro," "to divorce oneself from society, to exist without regrets, to set out on that uncharted journey into the imperatives of the self."

These days I'm coming around to my wife's view that it's not just okay but even virtuous to give less to humanity than Sartre, de Beauvoir, or Dostoevsky, that we just do what we can with the *donné*, the raw material of grey matter with which we have been endowed. But doesn't the lesser *donné* demand that we do more with it? Jean Paul, Simone, and Fyodor did not have to angst about the night of debauchery in Guadalajara when I could have read *The Idiot* or that book on Homer or studiously lingered on each page of the prints of Winslow Homer or firmed up in my mind that it was not Homer Winslow so as not to embarrass myself in the class I would teach. I should be satisfied too that my backseat affair on Avenida San Rafael with a subversive actress was as authentic as sleeping with Simone or buying a *Herald Tribune* from Jean Seberg.

What I have reported, in the end, with my two good eyes, though less cogent than what Sartre did with one good and one fish-like, stands, while much of his work he later renounced. If in the end you have little to say, you have nothing to recant. What after all is God if not a supreme editor?

GIFTS

My son and I are *on the road*, in a Mazda, and now it's my wife who is abroad. He asks what 4 times 7 is. I tell him. Moments later he tells me, with tears, that it will be 168 hours until he sees his mom again. It's baffling that he could do the latter calculation in his head and not the former. I'm tempted to say that the hours are easier than the days. And what he is dealing with is sadness, temporarily anesthetizing himself with calculation. It's not as if she is in detox or the slammer; just a vacation. But all he sees, like de Beauvoir, is the goneness.

And when his parents die? Calculate that simple mundane goneness. Sorting out the unsortable. We evolve, we are told, not with a purpose but with a direction; traits that are better suited for the environment to survive. Either sadness must be somehow good for the perpetuation of the species or it's a spandrel—Dan Dennett's icon for accidental by-product. So I'm wondering—if we could all be semi-Spocks, devoid of sadness—would we? Sadness persisting only as one of those multi-dimensions that physicists tell us exist but are unknowable? I'm thinking *no*, even though, ironically, the sadness I'm feeling over the excised, diminished self would be banished. Funny, though, to be, finally, sentimental about sadness.

The gift I most cherished from my father was a fake-pearl-handled knife with a silver horse head at the hilt and nicely-worked leather scabbard, from Mexico. Now, I'm getting my son a gift for graduating third grade, a jackknife, thinking it a rite of passage. He asks what it is for, and part of me wants to give back to him his sempiternal *duh*. I simply suggest that he go to the woodpile and make a bow and arrow.

"Dad, (*rolling eye affect*) you can buy that."

Indeed . . .

It makes me wonder what his trip will be like, *on the road 2027*, his Gua-*duh*-lajara, as he laughingly refers to my writing. We're almost in the Walmart parking lot when I spy a shingle saying "Karl *somebody*, Accountant." It is soliciting me who have never hired an accountant. I suppose that what they do is count. And I'm wondering what it is I might have numerous enough that I couldn't just as easily count it myself, that I would pay Karl to do it for me. The car parked, I stop a moment to take the question seriously, dismissing out of hand the notion of employing Karl as civic duty, to get the economy rolling again. I think what I have most of is time — if the units of calculation are small enough — for this I could use a man of Karl's expertise, to figure out my earthly allotment. I want to know because I want to spend it all, save timeouts for depression, with my son; and I recall four years back his gift to me — as we headed off to "school," — one rock, from his staircase collection ("nature" — he called it.)

— *Here, dad, so you won't forget me when I'm gone.*

AYDIN M. AKGÜN is a novelist and a poet. He was born and raised in Izmir, Turkey. He graduated from the Lycée Saint Joseph in Izmir and moved to the United States in 1995. He received his B.A. in both International Relations and French from the University of Nevada, Reno, in 2000, and his M.A. in Creative Writing in both poetry and fiction from Johns Hopkins University in 2009. His poems have been published in several literary journals — *Curating Alexandria*, *The Chicago Literary Review*, *Hotel Amerika*, and *Potomac Review*. He lives and works in Washington D.C.

ELLERY BECK is an undergraduate student majoring in English at Salisbury University. She was one of the winners of the 2019 AWP *Portland Review* flash contest. Her poems are published or forthcoming in *Crab Creek Review*, *Arkana*, *Little Patuxent Review*, *Thin Air Magazine*, *The Broadkill Review*, and elsewhere. She's the Interview Editor for *The Shore Poetry*.

A.M. BRANDT'S work can be found in *The Southern Review*, *The Sewanee Review*, *Spoon River Poetry Anthology*, *The National Poetry Review*, and *Parhelion Literary Magazine*, among others. She teaches writing and literature at Savannah College of Art and Design in Savannah, Georgia, where she lives with her husband and daughter.

Poet and photographer, **RONDA PISZK BROATCH** is the author of *Lake of Fallen Constellations* (MoonPath Press, 2015). Ronda was a finalist for the Four Way Books Prize, and her poems have been nominated several times for the Pushcart Prize. Her journal publications include *Blackbiard*, *Prairie Schooner*, *Sycamore Review*, *Mid-American Review*, *Puerto* *del Sol,* and Public Radio KUOW's *All Things Considered,* among others.

MARK BURKE'S work has appeared or is forthcoming in *North American Review, Beloit Poetry Journal, Sugar House Review, Nimrod International Journal,* and others. His work has recently been nominated for a Pushcart prize. See: markanthonyburkesongsandpoems.com.

MARISA P. CLARK is a queer writer from the South whose work has appeared in *Apalachee Review, Cream City Review, Foglifter, Ontario Review, Pilgrimage,* and elsewhere, with work forthcoming in *Shenandoah, Evening Street Review, Pangyrus, Pomme Journal, Rust + Moth,* and *Whale Road Review,* among others. She was twice the winner of the Agnes Scott College Writers' Festival Prizes (in fiction, 1996; in nonfiction, 1997), and *Best American Essays 2011* recognized her creative nonfiction among its Notable Essays. She reads fiction for *New England Review* and makes her home in New Mexico with three parrots and two dogs.

MICK COCHRANE grew up in St. Paul, MN, and currently lives in Buffalo, NY, where he teaches writing at Canisius College. He's published novels with Nan Talese/ Doubleday, St. Martin's, and Knopf Books for Young Readers, and his stories and poems have appeared in a number of magazines, including *The Sun, The Cincinnati Review, Five Points,* and *Southern Poetry Review.*

KAY COSGROVE & LAUREN HILGER have published their collaborative poetry in *Barrow Street, Cosmonauts Avenue, Denver Quarterly, New American Writing, Ninth Letter,* and *Washington Square,* among other journals. They have also presented on collaboration at Poetry by the Sea: A Global Conference and FRIEDA for generations. For more information, visit kaycosgrove.com and laurenhilger.com.

Timothy DeLizza lives in Baltimore, MD. During daytime hours, he's an energy attorney for the government. His novella *Jerry (from Accounting)* was published by Amazon.com's Day One imprint. His work can be found here: www.timothy-delizza.com.

Isolda Dosamantes was born in 1969 in Tlaxcala, Mexico, where she lives with her painter husband Katsumi Kurosaki and their son. She is the author of several collection of poetry, including *Paisaje sobre la seda* (2008), *Apuntes de viaje* (2012), and *Después del hambre* (2017). Her poetry can also be found in venues such as *AMP*, *The Bitter Oleander*, *Flyway*, *International Poetry Review*, and *La Canasta*.

Matt Duggan, born in Bristol, U.K., won the Erbacce Prize for Poetry in 2015 with his first collection, *Dystopia 38.10*. His work has been published in several journals, including *Ghost City Review*, *The Journal*, *Into the Void*, *Confluence*, *Marble Poetry Magazine*, *The Seventh Quarry*, *Harbinger Asylum*, and *Eyeflash Poetry Journal*. Matt was one of the winners of the Naji Naamans Literary Prize, and his second full collection, *Woodworm (3D)* (Hedgehog Poetry Press) was published in July 2019.

Andrea England is co-editor of the recently released anthology, *Scientists and Poets #Resist* (2019), and the author of *Other Geographies* (2017), and *Inventory of a Field* (2014). Her work has appeared widely in journals such as *Sonora Review*, *Fourteen Hills Review*, *Glass: A Journal of Poetry*, and others. She lives, writes, and teaches between Kalamazoo and Manistee, Michigan. To learn more about her life's work, visit andreajengland.com.

Bill Glose is a former paratrooper and combat platoon leader. The author of four poetry collections, Glose was named the Daily Press Poet Laureate in 2011 and featured by

NPR on *The Writer's Almanac* in 2017. His poems have appeared in numerous journals, including *The Missouri Review*, *Rattle*, *The Sun*, *Narrative Magazine*, and *Poet Lore*.

TRACY HAACK has an MFA from Western Washington University and an MA from Northern Michigan University. Her work has been published in *Fugue*, *The Pinch*, *Hobart*, and more. She works as a library assistant and lives with her husband and orange cat loaf named Benjamin Buttons.

ANN HILLESLAND'S work has been published in many literary journals, including *Fourth Genre*, *Sou'wester*, *Bayou*, *The Laurel Review*, *Corium*, and *SmokeLong Quarterly*. It has been selected for the *Wigleaf* Top 50 Very Short Fictions, nominated for a Pushcart Prize, and presented onstage by Stories on Stage. She is a graduate of the MFA program at Queen's University of Charlotte. Her website, including her blog about hats, is at annhillesland.com.

JESSICA HOLLANDER'S story collection *In These Times the Home Is a Tired Place* won the Katherine Anne Porter Prize and was published by the University of North Texas Press. Her stories have been published in many journals, such as *The Georgia Review*, *The Gettysburg Review*, *The Cincinnati Review*, *The Journal*, *Quarterly West*, *Hayden's Ferry Review*, *West Branch*, *Sonora Review*, and *Cimarron Review*. She received her MFA from the University of Alabama and is now an Assistant Professor at the University of Nebraska at Kearney.

ASHLEY ANNE HOWARD is an MFA candidate at the University of North Carolina Wilmington and a BFA graduate from Emerson College. Alongside her studies, she is copyeditor for *Ecotone* and a Graduate Teaching Assistant in the Creative Writing department at UNCW. She is currently working on a collection about ghosts, loss, and the space in between.

TOSHIYA KAMEI holds an MFA in Literary Translation from the University of Arkansas. His translations of Latin American literature include *My Father Thinks I'm a Fakir* by Claudia Apablaza, *Silent Herons* by Selfa Chew, and *The Torments of Aristarco* by Ana García Bergua.

KEVIN J. KELLEY'S writing has appeared in *The Massachusetts Review, Entropy, Thin Air Literary Magazine, Eastern Iowa Review,* and *High Country News.* He holds an MFA in Creative Writing from the University of Wyoming, and currently lives in Denver.

A graduate of Vassar College, SHARON KENNEDY-NOLLE holds an MFA and doctoral degree from the University of Iowa. These poems are part of a larger collection of elegies, *Black Wick,* written in memory of her oldest son. Sharon's poetry has appeared or is upcoming in *Potomac Review, Edison Literary Review, Qwerty, FRiGG, Prism, Zone 3, The Round, Chicago Quarterly Review, Juked, The Midwest Quarterly, Storyscape, Talking River,* and *Vox Poetica,* among others. Her dissertation was published as *Writing Reconstruction: Race, Gender, and Citizenship in the Postwar South* (University of North Carolina Press, 2015). Her chapbook *Black Wick* was a semi-finalist for the 2018 Tupelo Snowbound Chapbook Contest.

KEVIN KING is the author of the novels *All the Stars Came Out That Night* (Dutton, 2005) and *Phantom* (Open-bks, 2017). He is the recipient of a poetry fellowship (2007) from the New Hampshire State Council on the Arts and has published in numerous journals, including *Ploughshares, Stand, Threepenny Review,* etc.

DAN LEACH'S short fiction can be found in *The New Madrid Review, The Greensboro Review,* and *storySouth.* His debut collection, *Floods and Fires,* was released by University

Press of North Georgia in 2017. He is an MFA candidate at Warren Wilson.

LIZ MARLOW'S poems have appeared or are forthcoming in *The Carolina Quarterly, The Greensboro Review, The Rumpus, Silk Road Review,* and elsewhere.

JOSHUA MARTIN'S work has appeared or is forthcoming in *december, The Carolina Quarterly, Crab Orchard Review, Nashville Review, Raleigh Review, Asheville Poetry Review, Salamander, Borderlands: The Texas Poetry Review, The Cortland Review,* and elsewhere. He won third place in the 2019 William Matthews Poetry Contest, was a finalist in the 2019 Atticus Review Contest, the 2019 Gemini Contest, the 2017 Nazim Hikmet Contest, and he won a fellowship to the 2019 Martha's Vineyard Institute of Creative Writing. He is a PhD student in creative writing at Georgia State University and is currently working on his manuscript.

CAROL MATOS' debut collection of poems, *The Hush Before the Animals Attack,* was published by Main Street Rag in 2013. Her poetry has appeared in *34th Parallel, Zone 3, The Comstock Review, ROOM, The Prose-Poem Project, Columbia Journal, RHINO,* and *The Chattahoochee Review.* She has been a semifinalist for the *Spoon River Poetry Review* Editors' Prize, and a nominee for the Pushcart Poetry Prize. Formerly a professional photographer with exhibitions in New York City and Europe, she now serves as Vice President for Administration at Manhattan School of Music.

V.C. MCCABE is an Appalachian poet and the author of *Give the Bard a Tetanus Shot* (Vegetarian Alcoholic Press, 2019). Her work has been featured in exhibits and many journals worldwide, including the Kurt Vonnegut Memorial

Museum & Library, FRANK Gallery, *Prairie Schooner*, *The Minnesota Review*, *Poet Lore*, *Appalachian Heritage*, *Tar River Poetry*, and *Spillway*. She has lived in Ireland and West Virginia. Her website is vcmccabe.com.

CAMERON MORSE lives with his wife Lili and son Theodore in Blue Springs, Missouri. He was diagnosed with a glioblastoma in 2014. With a 14.6 month life expectancy, he entered the Creative Writing program at the University of Missouri — Kansas City and, in 2018, graduated with an M.F.A. His poems have been published in numerous magazines, including *New Letters*, *Bridge Eight*, and *South Dakota Review*. His first collection, *Fall Risk*, won Glass Lyre Press's 2018 Best Book Award. His second, *Father Me Again*, is available from Spartan Press.

RAYNALD PATRICE DESMEULES NAYLER'S work has been published in the *Beloit Poetry Journal*, *Sentence*, *Weave*, *The Berkeley Fiction Review*, and many other journals. He is a Foreign Service Officer and a Russian speaker. He has worked in Russia, Central Asia, Afghanistan, and the Caucasus for over a decade. His most recent posting was as Press Attaché in Baku, Azerbaijan. His current posting is to Pristina, Kosovo as Cultural Attaché.

JOHN A. NIEVES has poems forthcoming or recently published in journals such as: *North American Review*, *Poetry Northwest*, *Southern Review*, *32 Poems*, and *Copper Nickel*. He won the *Indiana Review* Poetry Contest and his first book, *Curio*, won the Elixir Press Annual Poetry Award Judge's Prize. He is associate professor of English at Salisbury University and an editor of *The Shore Poetry*. He received his M.A. from University of South Florida and his Ph.D. from the University of Missouri.

ANN QUINN'S poetry was selected by Stanley Plumly as first place winner in the 2015 Bethesda Literary Arts Festival poetry contest, and has been nominated for a Pushcart Prize. Her work is published in *Little Patuxent Review, Broadkill Review, The Ekphrastic Review,* and other journals, and is included in the anthology *Red Sky: Poetry on the Global Epidemic of Violence Against Women.* Ann lives in Catonsville, Maryland with her family, where she teaches reflective and creative writing and music and plays clarinet with the Columbia Orchestra. Her degrees are in music performance; she fell in love with poetry in mid-life. Her chapbook, *Final Deployment,* is published by Finishing Line Press. Please visit online at www. annquinn.net.

SARAH MOLLIE SILBERMAN holds an MFA from George Mason University and lives in Washington, DC. Her stories have appeared in *Booth, CutBank, Juked, Nashville Review, New South, Puerto del Sol, Witness,* and elsewhere. Find her online at www.sarahmolliesilberman.com.

MATTHEW SUMPTER is the author of the poetry collection *Public Land* (University of Tampa Press, 2018), which won the Anita Claire Scharf Award. His poems have appeared or are forthcoming in *The New Yorker, The New Republic, AGNI,* and *Poetry Daily.* His creative prose has appeared in *Glimmer Train* and *Pithead Chapel.* He is a Visiting Assistant Professor in the English Department at Tulane University.

JOHN SIBLEY WILLIAMS is the author of *As One Fire Consumes Another* (Orison Poetry Prize, 2019), *Skin Memory* (Backwaters Prize, University of Nebraska Press, 2019), *Disinheritance,* and *Controlled Hallucinations.* A nineteen-time Pushcart nominee, John is the winner of numerous awards, including the Wabash Prize for Poetry, Philip Booth Award, *American Literary Review* Poetry Contest, Phyllis Smart-Young Prize, Nancy D. Hargrove Editors' Prize, *Confrontation* Poetry Prize, and Laux/Millar Prize. He serves as editor of *The Inflectionist Review* and works as a literary agent. Previous publishing credits include: *The Yale Review, Midwest Quarterly, Southern Review, Sycamore Review, Prairie Schooner, The Massachusetts Review, Poet Lore, Saranac Review, Atlanta Review, TriQuarterly, Columbia Poetry Review, Mid-American Review, Poetry Northwest, Third Coast*, and various anthologies. He lives in Portland, Oregon.

Acknowledgements

V.C. McCabe's "Solastalgia" first appeared in her collection, *Give the Bard a Tetanus Shot* (Vegetarian Alcoholic Press, 2019).